Volney Streamer

Voices of Doubt and Trust

Volney Streamer

Voices of Doubt and Trust

ISBN/EAN: 9783337362638

Printed in Europe, USA, Canada, Australia, Japan

Cover: Foto ©Andreas Hilbeck / pixelio.de

More available books at **www.hansebooks.com**

Voices

of

Doubt and Trust

Selected by

Volney Streamer

NEW YORK
BRENTANO'S
1897

Contents

NOTE

THE compiler wishes to express his obligations to the following publishers, who have most generously allowed selections to be made from the authors on their lists: Messrs. D. Appleton & Co.; The Bowen-Merrill Company; George H. Ellis; C. P. Farrell; Houghton, Mifflin & Co.; P. J. Kennedy; Lee & Shepard; The Macmillan Company; George P. Putnam's Sons; Roberts Brothers; Charles Scribner's Sons; Frederick A. Stokes Company, and Stone & Kimball.

Thanks are especially due to the following authors, who have with uniform courtesy personally given permission for this use of their writings: Messrs. Thomas Bailey Aldrich, John Vance Cheney, William Dean Howells, William James, George Klingle, Josiah Royce, Goldwin Smith, and Richard Henry Stoddard; also to Horace L. Traubel, who has allowed three selections to be made from the works of the late Walt Whitman, and to Mrs. Helen M. Reeve Aldrich for permitting the reprinting of a poem by her gifted daughter, the late Anne Reeve Aldrich.

FOREWORD

THIS little book makes no aim to fill a gap in Literature; but it is believed that no attempt has previously been made to collect under one cover such candid expressions of a Soul's search for Truth, ranging from the darkness of hopeless Doubt to that radiance that fills the heart in sublimest Trust. It is conceded, by most people, that the honest and sincere expression of opinion—whether one holds with it or not—is entitled to a respectful hearing. Many voices have spoken in no uncertain tones, and many weary Seekers along Life's dusty way have been cheered by the faintly echoed hope voiced by another Seeker a little in advance. The collector's one earnest desire has been to give to a larger audience certain of these clear, strong words that have been hitherto sounded for the few only, owing to the manner in which they were published, or remained unpublished. And he trusts that, even in this brief volume, the casual reader will perhaps find some new thought, or some new expression of an older hope, that may revive his sinking courage, or give him a moment of cheer.

Foreword

As nearly as was practical a regular sequence has been maintained along the line of thought the book intends to express, and in every instance the author's own words are scrupulously given, and the thought entire ; wherever extracts have been made, the utmost care has been taken that abridgment in no way obscures the author's exact meaning, and there is no attempt made to edit these selections—they explain themselves and require no interpreter. There has been but little culled along the beaten paths, but there are certain favorites that will be looked for in such a collection, and can scarcely be omitted. Many most suitable selections were reluctantly laid aside from lack of space in the limits set for the work.

But the intrinsic value of the music is the thing which must hold the audience ; without it the most elaborately printed program would not avail ; so shall we allow the voices to speak, each after its own manner and degree ?

V. S.

New York, July 19, 1897

Authors and Titles

Authors and Titles

Authors and Titles

Authors and Titles

Authors and Titles

Authors and Titles

Authors and Titles

Authors and Titles

Authors and Titles

Authors and Titles

Authors and Titles

Questionings

Truth never can be confirmed enough,
Though doubts did ever sleep.

SHAKSPERE

MORTALITY

I said in my heart it is because of the sons of men, that God may prove them, and that they may see that they themselves are beasts. For that which befalleth the sons of men befalleth beasts ; even one thing befalleth them. As the one dieth, so dieth the other; yea, they have all one breath ; and man hath no pre-eminence above the beasts : for all is vanity. All go unto one place ; all are of the dust, and all turn to dust again. Who knoweth the spirit of man whether it goeth upward, and the spirit of the beast whether it goeth downward to the earth ? Wherefore I saw that there is nothing better, than that a man should rejoice in his own works; for that is his portion : for who shall bring him back to see what shall be after him ?

ECCLESIASTES

THE HINDU SCEPTIC

I THINK till I weary with thinking
    (Said the sad-eyed Hindu King),
And I see but shadows around me,
    Illusion in every thing.

How knowest thou aught of God,
    Of his favor, or of his wrath ?
Can the little fish tell what the lion thinks,
    Or map out the eagle's path ?

Can the finite the Infinite search ?
    Did the blind discover the stars ?
Is the thought I think a thought,
    Or a throb of my brain in its bars ?

For aught my eye can discern,
    Your God is what you think good,—
Yourself flashed back from the glass
    When the light pours on it in flood.

You preach to me to be just,
    And this is his realm, you say,
And the good are dying of hunger,
    While the bad gorge every day.

3

An Agnostic's Apology

You say that he loveth mercy,
  And the famine is not yet gone ;
That he hateth the shedder of blood,
  Yet he slayeth us every one.

You say that my soul shall live,
  That the spirit can never die,—
If he was content when I was not,
  Why not when I have passed by ?

You say I must have a meaning,—
  So must dung, and its meaning is flowers ;
What if our souls are but nurture
  For lives that are higher than ours ?

When the fish swims out of the water,
  When the birds soar out of the blue,
Man's thought may transcend man's knowledge
And your God be no reflex of you.

                                   SIR ALFRED LYALL

AN AGNOSTIC'S APOLOGY

ONE insoluble doubt has haunted men's minds since thought began in the world. No answer has ever been suggested. One school of philosophers hands it to the next. It is denied in one form only to reappear in another. The question is not which system excludes the doubt, but how it expresses the doubt. Admit or deny the competence of reason in theory, we all agree that it fails in practice. Theologians revile reason as much as Agnostics ; they then appeal to it and it decides against them.   They amend their plea by excluding certain questions from its jurisdiction, and those questions include the whole difficulty.   They go to revelation, and revelation replies by calling doubt mystery.   They declare that their consciousness declares just what they want it to declare.   Ours declares something else.   Who is to decide ?   The only appeal is to experience, and to appeal to experience is to admit the fundamental dogma of Agnosticism.

Is it not, then, the very height of audacity, in face of a difficulty, which meets us at every turn, which has perplexed all the ablest thinkers in proportion to their ability, which vanishes in one shape only to show itself in another, to declare roundly, not only that the difficulty can be solved, but that it does not exist ?   Why, when no honest man will deny in private that every ultimate problem is wrapped in the profoundest mystery, do honest men proclaim in pulpits that unhesitating certainty is the duty of the most foolish and ignorant ?   Is it not a spectacle to make the angels laugh ?   We are a company of ignorant beings, feeling our way through mists and darkness, learning only by incessantly-repeated blunders, obtaining a glimmering of truth by falling into every conceivable error, dimly discerning light enough for our daily needs, but hopelessly differing whenever we attempt to describe the ultimate origin or end of our paths ; and yet, when one of us ventures to declare that we don't know the map of the universe as well as the map of our infinitesimal parish, he is hooted, reviled, and perhaps told that he will be damned to all eternity for his faithlessness. Amidst all the endless and hopeless controversies which have left nothing but bare husks of meaningless words, we have been able to discover certain reliable truths. They don't take us very far, and the condition of discovering them has been distrust of *à priori* guesses, and the systematic interrogation of experience. Let us, say some of us, follow at least this clue. Here we shall find sufficient guidance for the needs of life, though we renounce forever the attempt to get behind the veil which no one has succeeded in raising ; if, indeed, there be anything behind. You miserable Agnostics ! is the retort ; throw aside such rubbish and cling to the old husks. Stick to the words which profess to explain everything ; call your doubts mysteries, and they won't disturb you any longer ; and believe in those necessary truths of which no two philosophers have ever succeeded in giving the same version.

Gentlemen, we can only reply, wait till you have some show of agreement among yourselves. Wait till you can give some answer, not palpably a verbal answer, to some of the doubts which oppress us as they oppress you. Wait till you can point to some single truth, however trifling, which has been discovered by your method, and will stand the test of discussion and verification. Wait till you can appeal to reason without in the same breath vilifying reason. Wait till your Divine revelations have something more to reveal than the hope that the hideous doubts which they sug-

gest may possibly be without foundation. Till then
we shall be content to admit openly, what you whisper
under your breath or hide in technical jargon, that the
ancient secret is a secret still ; that man knows nothing
of the Infinite and Absolute ; and that, knowing nothing, he had better not be dogmatic about his ignorance.
And, meanwhile, we will endeavor to be as charitable
as possible, and whilst you trumpet forth officially your
contempt for scepticism, we will at least try to believe
that you are imposed upon by your own bluster.

LESLIE STEPHEN

CLAUDIO AND THE DUKE

DUKE.   Be absolute for death ; either death or
      life
Shall thereby be the sweeter.   Reason thus with life :
If I do lose thee, I do lose a thing
That none but fools would keep : a breath thou art,
Servile to all the skyey influences,
That dost this habitation, where thou keep'st,
Hourly afflict : merely, thou art death's fool ;
For him thou labor'st by thy flight to shun,
And yet runn'st toward him still.   Thou art not noble ;
For all the accommodations that thou bear'st
Are nursed by baseness.   Thou art by no means valiant ;
For thou dost fear the soft and tender fork
Of a poor worm.   Thy best of rest is sleep,
And that thou oft provokest ; yet grossly fear'st
Thy death, which is no more.   Thou art not thyself ;

Claudio and the Duke

For thou exist'st on many a thousand grains
That issue out of dust.   Happy thou art not ;
For what thou hast not, still thou strivest to get,
And what thou hast, forget'st.   Thou are not certain ;
For thy complexion shifts to strange effects,
After the moon.   If thou art rich, thou art poor ;
For, like an ass whose back with ingots bows,
Thou bear'st thy heavy riches but a journey,
And death unloads thee.   Friend hast thou none ;
For thine own bowels, which do call thee sire,
The mere effusion of thy proper loins,
Do curse the gout, serpigo, and the rheum,
For ending thee no sooner.   Thou hast nor youth, nor
    age ;
But, as it were, an after-dinner's sleep,
Dreaming on both ; for all thy blessed youth
Becomes as aged, and doth beg the alms
Of palsied eld ; and when thou art old and rich,
Thou hast neither heat, affection, limb, nor beauty,
To make thy riches pleasant.   What's yet in this
That bears the name of life ?   Yet in this life
Lie hid moe thousand deaths : yet death we fear,
That makes these odds all even.

CLAUDIO.   Ay, but to die, and go we know not where ;
To lie in cold obstruction and to rot ;
This sensible warm motion to become
A kneaded clod ; and the delighted spirit
To bathe in fiery floods, or to reside
In thrilling region of thick-ribbed ice ;

My Slain

To be imprison'd in the viewless winds,
And blown with restless violence round about
The pendent world ; or to be worse than worst
Of those that lawless and incertain thoughts
Imagine howling :—'tis too horrible !
The weariest and most loathed worldly life,
That age, ache, penury, and imprisonment
Can lay on nature, is a paradise
To what we fear of death.

SHAKSPERE
Measure for Measure

MY SLAIN

THIS sweet child which hath climbed upon my
        knee,
  This amber-haired, four-summered little maid,
With her unconscious beauty troubleth me,
  With her low prattle maketh me afraid.
Ah, darling ! when you cling and nestle so
  You hurt me though you do not see me cry,
  Nor hear the weariness with which I sigh,
For the dear babe I killed so long ago.
  I tremble at the touch of your caress;
I am not worthy of your innocent faith;
  I who with whetted knives of worldliness
Did put my own child-heartedness to death,
  Beside whose grave I pace forevermore,
  Like desolation on a shipwrecked shore.

My Slain

There is no little child within me now
    To sing back to the thrushes, to leap up
When June winds kiss me, when an apple-bough
    Laughs into blossoms, or a buttercup
Plays with the sunshine, or a violet
    Dances in the glad dew.   Alas ! alas !
    The meaning of the daisies in the grass
I have forgotten; and if my cheeks are wet,
    It is not with the blitheness of the child,
But with the bitter sorrow of past years.
    O moaning life, with life irreconciled;
O backward-looking thought, O pain, O tears,
    For us there is not any silver sound
    Of rhythmic wonders springing from the ground.

Woe worth the knowledge and the bookish lore
    Which makes men mummies, weighs out every grain
Of that which was miraculous before,
    And sneers the heart down with the scoffing brain;
Woe worth the peering, analytic days
    That dry the tender juices in the breast
    And put the thunders of the Lord to test,
So that no marvel must be, and no praise,
    Nor any God except necessity.
What can ye give my poor starved life in lieu
    Of this dead cherub which I slew for ye ?
Take back your doubtful wisdom, and renew
    My early, foolish freshness of the dunce,
    Whose simple instincts guessed the heavens at once.

RICHARD REALF

THE SOUL AND THE FUTURE LIFE

A reply to Frederic Harrison.   (*See Section Third*)

I UNDERSTAND and I respect the meaning of the word "soul," as used by Pagan and Christian philosophers for what they believe to be the imperishable seat of human personality, bearing throughout eternity its burden of woe, or its capacity for adoration and love.   I confess that my dull moral sense does not enable me to see anything base or selfish in the desire for a future life among the spirits of the just made perfect ; or even among a few such poor fallible souls as one has known here below.   And if I am not satisfied with the evidence which is offered me that such a soul and such a future life exist, I am content to take what is to be had and to make the best of the brief span of existence that is within my reach, without reviling those whose faith is more robust and whose hopes are richer and fuller.   But in the interest of scientific clearness, I object to say that I have a soul, when I mean, all the while, that my organism has certain mental functions which, like the rest, are dependent upon its molecular composition, and come to an end when I die ; and I object still more to affirm that I look to a future life, when all that I mean is, that the influence of my sayings and doings will be more or less felt by a number of people after the physical components of that organism are scattered to the four winds.

" Our Little Life "

Throw a stone into the sea, and there is a sense in which it is true that the wavelets which spread around it have an effect through all space and all time.   Shall we say that the stone has a future life ?

It is not worth while to have broken away, not without pain and grief, from beliefs which, true or false, embody great and fruitful conceptions, to fall back into the arms of a half-breed between science and theology endowed, like most half-breeds, with the faults of both parents and the virtues of neither.   It is unwise by such a lapse to expose one's self to the temptation of holding with the hare and hunting with the hounds—of using the weapons of one progenitor to damage the other.   THOMAS HENRY HUXLEY

"OUR LITTLE LIFE"

THE Worldly Hope men set their Hearts upon
    Turns Ashes—or it prospers ; and anon,
Like Snow upon the Desert's dusty Face,
Lighting a little hour or two—was gone.

Think, in this batter'd Caravanserai
Whose Portals are alternate Night and Day,
    How Sultán after Sultán with his Pomp
Abode his destin'd Hour, and went his way.

For Some we loved, the loveliest and the best
That from his Vintage rolling Time has prest,
    Have drunk their Cup a Round or two before,
And one by one crept silently to rest.

" Our Little Life "

And we, that now make merry in the Room
They left, and Summer dresses in new bloom,
   Ourselves must we beneath the Couch of Earth
Descend—ourselves to make a Couch—for whom ?

Ah, make the most of what we yet may spend,
Before we too into the Dust descend ;
   Dust into Dust, and under Dust, to lie
Sans Wine, sans Song, sans Singer, and—sans End!

Why, all the Saints and Sages who discuss'd
Of the Two Worlds so learnedly are thrust
   Like foolish Prophets forth ; their Words to Scorn
Are scatter'd, and their Mouths are stopt with Dust.

Myself when young did eagerly frequent
Doctor and Saint, and heard great argument
   About it and about : but evermore
Came out by the same door where in I went.

With them the seed of Wisdom did I sow,
And with my own hand wrought to make it grow ;
   And this was all the Harvest that I reap'd—
" I came like Water, and like Wind I go."

Into this Universe, and *Why* not knowing,
Nor *Whence*, like Water willy-nilly flowing ;
   And out of it, as Wind along the Waste,
I know not *Whither*, willy-nilly blowing.

What, without asking, hither hurried *Whence ?*
And, without asking, *Whither* hurried hence !

" Our Little Life "

Oh, many a Cup of this forbidden Wine
Must drown the memory of that insolence !

And fear not lest Existence closing your
Account, and mine, should know the like no more ;
  The Eternal Sáki from that Bowl has pour'd
Millions of Bubbles like us, and will pour.

When You and I behind the Veil are past,
Oh but the long long while the World shall last,
  Which of our Coming and Departure heeds
As the SEV'N SEAS should heed a pebble cast.

A Moment's Halt—a momentary taste
Of BEING from the Well amid the Waste—
  And Lo !—the phantom Caravan has reach'd
The NOTHING it set out from—Oh, make haste !

Would you that Spangle of Existence spend
About THE SECRET—quick about it, Friend !
  A Hair perhaps divides the False and True—
And upon what, prithee, does Life depend ?

O threats of Hell and hopes of Paradise !
One thing at least is certain,—*This* Life flies ;
  One thing is certain and the rest is Lies ;
The Flower that once has blown forever dies.

Strange, is it not ? that of the myriads who
Before us pass'd the door of Darkness through
  Not one returns to tell us of the Road,
Which to discover we must travel too.

"Our Little Life"

The Revelations of Devout and Learn'd
Who rose before us, and as Prophets burn'd,
   Are all but Stories, which, awoke from Sleep
They told their fellows, and to Sleep return'd.

I sent my Soul through the Invisible,
Some letter of that After-life to spell ;
   And by and by my Soul return'd to me,
And answer'd, "I Myself am Heav'n and Hell."

Heav'n but the Vision of fulfill'd Desire,
And Hell the Shadow of a Soul on fire,
   Cast on the Darkness into which Ourselves,
So late emerg'd from, shall so soon expire.

We are no other than a moving row
Of Magic shadow-shapes that come and go
   Round with this Sun-illumin'd Lantern held
In Midnight by the Master of the Show ;

Impotent Pieces of the Game He plays
Upon this Checker-board of Nights and Days ;
   Hither and thither moves, and checks, and slays,
And one by one back in the Closet lays.

The Ball no question makes of Ayes and Noes,
But Right or Left as strikes the Player goes ;
   And He that toss'd you down into the Field,
He knows about it all—HE knows—HE knows !

The Moving Finger writes ; and having writ,
Moves on : nor all your Piety nor Wit

" Our Little Life "

Shall lure it back to cancel half a Line,
Nor all your Tears wash out a Word of it.

And that inverted Bowl they call the Sky,
Whereunder crawling coop'd we live and die,
    Lift not your hands to *It* for help—for It
As impotently rolls as you or I.

What ! out of senseless Nothing to provoke
A Conscious Something to resent the Yoke
    Of unpermitted Pleasure, under pain
Of Everlasting Penalties, if broke !

What, from his helpless Creature be repaid
Pure Gold for what he lent us dross-allay'd—
    Sue for a Debt we never did contract,
And cannot answer—Oh the sorry trade !

Oh Thou, who didst with pitfall and with gin
Beset the Road I was to wander in,
    Thou wilt not with Predestin'd Evil round
Emmesh, and then impute my Fall to Sin !

Oh Thou, who Man of baser Earth didst make
And ev'n with Paradise devise the Snake ;
    For all the Sin wherewith the Face of Man
Is blacken'd—Man's Forgiveness give—and take !

OMAR KHAYYÁM

RUBAIYAT, Translated by Edward Fitzgerald

" ARE God and Nature then at strife?" asks Tennyson. The question illuminates one of the most striking chapters in human thought. When we trace the history of the idea of God as it probably arose in the mind of early man, we find that it stands for his crude theory of a Spirit which caused Nature to be, which he believed to control and actuate the forces of sun and air, storm and pestilence. These views, from their elevation of subject, unwarrantably gained a sacredness of character which made them rigid, almost unchangeable. Hence the idea of the Divine Personality and Government has hung farther and farther behind man's advancing knowledge of Nature— that knowledge from which, in its first poor estate, his idea of God was derived. At last, God and Nature are imagined "At Strife." But what should be the idea of God here and now but an answer to the question, What kind of Being would make and conduct such a universe as this? The degree of verity in this idea of God would plainly depend upon the fullness of the knowledge of Nature whence it would proceed, the degree of completeness with which that knowledge would be co-ordinated and unified. Very different from such an idea of God is the idea of Him inherited from men who lived thousands of years ago in the ignorance and moral poverty then inevitable. The conflict between theology and science proves indeed to be little else than the discord between new knowledge and old guesses.

But why not dispense with the idea of God altogether ? We have ceased to believe that He interferes with the order of Nature : let us endeavor to learn what that order is and abide by it. Let us reason directly from facts known to facts unknown and probable, without the refraction unavoidable when a hypothetical Person (abstracted after all from known facts) is brought into the case. What after all does God do, that Science does not enable us to know, or to predict with increasing probability ? Why make a Mirror of Nature, liable to limitation and warp, when Nature bids us look immediately upon her face ?

FRANCIS JOHN BELL

MEDITATIONS OF A HINDU PRINCE

ALL the world over, I wonder, in lands that I
　　　never have trod,
Are the people eternally seeking for the signs and
　　steps of a God ?
Westward across the ocean, and northward ayont the
　　snow,
Do they all stand gazing, as ever, and what do the
　　wisest know ?

Here, in this mystical India, the deities hover and
　　swarm
Like the wild bees heard in the tree tops, or the gusts
　　of a gathering storm;

18

Meditations of a Hindu Prince

In the air men hear their voices, their feet on the rocks
    are seen,
Yet we all say, " Whence is the message, and what
    may the wonders mean ? "

A million shrines stand open, and ever the censer
    swings,
As they bow to a mystical symbol, or the figures of
    ancient kings;
And the incense rises ever, and rises the endless cry
Of those who are heavy laden, and of cowards loth to
    die.

For the Destiny drives us together, like deer in a pass
    of the hills;
Above is the sky, and around us the sound of the shot
    that kills;
Pushed by a Power we see not, and struck by a hand
    unknown,
We pray to the trees for shelter, and press our lips to
    a stone.

The trees wave a shadowy answer, and the rock frowns
    hollow and grim,
And the form and the nod of the demon are caught in
    the twilight dim;
And we look to the starlight falling afar on the moun-
    tain crest—
Is there never a path runs upward to a refuge there
    and a rest ?

Meditations of a Hindu Prince

The path, ah ! who has shown it, and which is the
    faithful guide ?
The haven, ah ! who has known it ? for steep is the
    mountain side,
Forever the shot strikes surely, and ever the wasted
    breath
Of the praying multitude rises, whose answer is only
    death.

Here are the tombs of my kinsfolk, the fruit of an an-
    cient name,
Chiefs who were slain on the war-field, and women who
    died in flame ;
They are gods, these kings of the foretime, they are
    spirits who guard our race :
Ever I watch and worship ; they sit with a marble
    face.

And the myriad idols around me, and the legion of
    muttering priests,
The revels and rites unholy, the dark, unspeakable
    feasts !
What have they wrung from the Silence ?   Hath even
    a whisper come
Of the secret, Whence and Whither ?   Alas ! for the
    gods are dumb.

Shall I list to the words of the English, who come
    from the uttermost sea ?
" The Secret, hath it been told you, and what is your
    message to me ? "

Meditations of a Hindu Prince

It is nought but the world-wide story how the earth
    and the heavens began,
How the gods are glad and angry, and a Deity once
    was a man.

I had thought, "Perchance in the cities where the
    rulers of India dwell,
Whose orders flash from the far land, who girdle the
    earth with a spell,
They have fathom'd the depths we float on, or measured
    the unknown main—"
Sadly they turn from the venture, and say that the
    quest is vain.

Is life, then, a dream and delusion, and where shall the
    dreamer awake?
Is the world seen like shadows on water, and what if
    the mirror break?
Shall it pass like a camp that is struck, as a tent that
    is gathered and gone
From the sands that were lamp-lit at eve, and at morn-
    ing are level and lone?

Is there nought in the heaven above, whence the hail
    and the levin are hurl'd,
But the wind that is swept around us by the rush of the
    rolling world?
The wind that shall scatter my ashes, and bear me to
    silence and sleep
With the dirge, and the sounds of lamenting, and voices
    of women who weep?

SIR ALFRED LYALL

"O BROTHERS of sad lives ! they are so brief ;
    A few short years must bring us all relief :
Can we not bear these years of laboring breath ?
But if you would not this poor life fulfil,
Lo, you are free to end it when you will,
    Without the fear of waking after death."

.   .   .   .

Our shadowy congregation rested still,
    As musing on that message we had heard,
And brooding on that; ' End it when you will;'
    Perchance awaiting yet some other word ;
When keen as lightning through a muffled sky
Sprang forth a shrill and lamentable cry :—

"The man speaks sooth, alas ! the man speaks sooth ;
    We have no personal life beyond the grave ;
There is no God ; there is no wrath nor ruth :
    Can I find here the comfort which I crave ?

" In all eternity I had one chance,
    One few years' term of gracious human life :
The splendors of the intellect's advance,
    The sweetness of the home with babes and wife ;

.   .   .   .

"The rapture of mere being, full of health ;
    The careless childhood and the ardent youth,
The strenuous manhood winning various wealth,
    The reverend age serene with life's long truth :

The City of Dreadful Night

" All the sublime prerogatives of Man ;
  The storied memories of the times of old,
The patient tracking of the world's great plan
  Through sequences and changes myriadfold.

" This chance was never offered me before ;
  For me the infinite Past is blank and dumb :
This chance recurreth never, nevermore ;
  Blank, blank for me the infinite To-come.

.   .   .   .

" Speak not of comfort where no comfort is,
  Speak not at all : can words make foul things fair ?
Our life's a cheat, our death a black abyss :
  Hush, and be mute, envisaging despair."

This vehement voice came from the northern aisle,
  Rapid and shrill to its abrupt, harsh close ;
And none gave answer for a certain while,
  For words must shrink from these most wordless woes;
At last the pulpit speaker simply said,
With humid eyes, and thoughtful, drooping head,—

" My Brother, my poor Brothers, it is thus ;
This life holds nothing good for us,
  But it ends soon and nevermore can be ;
And we knew nothing of it ere our birth,
And shall know nothing when consigned to earth :
  I ponder these thoughts and they comfort me."

JAMES THOMSON

THE ICONOCLAST

A THOUSAND years shall come and go,
    A thousand years of night and day,
And man, through all their changing show,
    His tragic drama still shall play.

Ruled by some fond ideal's power,
    Cheated by passion or despair,
Still shall he waste life's trembling hour,
    In worship vain, and useless prayer.

Ah! where are they who rose in might,
    Who fired the temple and the shrine,
And hurled through Earth's Chaotic Night,
    The helpless gods it deemed divine?

Cease, longing soul, thy vain desire!
    What idol, in its stainless prime,
But falls, untouched of ax or fire,
    Before the steady eyes of Time?

He looks, and lo! our altars fall,
    The shrine reveals its gilded clay,
With decent hands we spread the pall,
    And, cold with wisdom, glide away.

Oh, where were courage, faith, and truth,
    If man went wandering all his day
In golden clouds of love and youth,
    Nor knew that both his steps betray?

Come, Time, while here we sit and wait,
    Be faithful, spoiler, to thy trust!
No death can further desolate
    The soul that knows its god was dust.

ROSE TERRY COOKE

IF DEATH ENDS ALL

AND suppose, after all, that death does end all. Next to eternal joy, next to being forever with those we love and those who have loved us—next to that, is to be wrapped in the dreamless drapery of eternal peace. Next to eternal life is eternal sleep. Upon the shadowy shore of death the sea of trouble casts no wave. Eyes that have been curtained by the everlasting dark will never know again the burning touch of tears. Lips touched by eternal silence will never speak again the broken words of grief. Hearts of dust do not break. The dead do not weep. Within the tomb no veiled and weeping sorrow sits. And in the rayless gloom is crouched no shuddering fear.

I had rather think of those I have loved, and lost, as having returned to earth, as having become a part of the elemental wealth of the world ; I would rather think of them as unconscious dust ; I would rather think of them as gurgling in the stream, floating in the clouds, bursting in light upon the shores of other worlds ; I would rather think of them as the lost visions of a forgotten night, than to have even the faintest fear that their naked souls have been clutched by an orthodox god. But as for me, I will leave the dead where nature leaves them. Whatever flower of hope springs in my heart I will cherish ; I will give it breath of sighs and rain of tears.

ROBERT G. INGERSOLL
Prose Poems

A DIALOGUE

THE Alpine summits—a complete chain of steep precipices, right in the heart of the Alps. Over the mountains is a pale-green, clear, silent sky. Hard, biting frost; firm, sparkling snow; dark, weather-beaten, ice-bound crags rise from beneath the snow.

Two colossi, two giants, rise from the horizon on either side—the Jungfrau and the Finsteraarhorn.

And the Jungfrau asks her neighbor : "What is the news? You can see better ; what is going on down there?"

Thousands of years pass by—as one moment. And Finsteraarhorn thunders back the answer : "Impenetrable clouds veil the earth. . . wait!"

Again thousands of years pass—as one moment.

"Well, what now?" asks the Jungfrau.

"Now, see : everything there is unchanged, confused, and petty. Blue water, dark woods, heaped up masses of gray stone, with those little insects running all about, you know—the two-legged ones which have never yet intruded upon your summit or mine."

"Men?"

"Yes, men."

Again thousands of years pass by— as a moment.

"Well, what now?" asks the Jungfrau.

"It seems to me as if fewer of those insects are to be seen," thunders Finsteraarhorn—"It's getting clearer down there—the waters narrower, the woods thinner."

Again thousands of years pass by—like one moment.

"What do you see now?" asks the Jungfrau.

"Round about us, near by, it seems to have got clearer," answered Finsteraarhorn; "but down there, in the distance, in the valleys there are still some spots, and something moving."

"And now?" asks the Jungfrau, after thousands of years more—a mere moment.

"Now all is well," answered Finsteraarhorn—"clear and shining everywhere: pure white wherever you look. . . . Our snow everywhere, nothing but snow and ice. All is frozen. All is calm and peaceful."

"Yes, now it is well!" answers the Jungfrau; "but we have talked enough, old friend. Let us sleep awhile."

"Yes, it is time we did."

They sleep, the giant mountains. The clear green sky above the ever-silent earth.

IVAN TURGENEV

Poems in prose

IF THIS WERE FAITH

GOD, if this were enough,
    That I see things bare to the buff
And up to the buttocks in mire;
That I ask nor hope nor hire,

If This Were Faith

Nut in the husk,
Nor dawn beyond the dusk,
Nor life beyond death ;
God, if this were faith ?

Having felt thy wind in my face
Spit sorrow and disgrace,
Having seen thine evil doom
In Golgotha and Khartoum,
And the brutes, the work of thine hands,
Fill with injustice lands
And stain with blood the sea :
If still in my veins the glee
Of the black night and the sun
And the lost battle run :
If, an adept,
The iniquitous lists I still accept
With joy, and joy to endure and be withstood,
And still to battle and perish for a dream of good :
God, if that were enough ?

If to feel, in the ink of the slough,
And the sink of the mire,
Veins of glory and fire
Run through and transpierce and transpire,
And a secret purpose of glory in every part,
And the answering glory of battle fill my heart,
To thrill with the joy of girded men
To go on forever and fail, and go on again,
And be mauled to the earth and arise,

Take Me, Mother Earth

And contend for the shade of a word and a thing not
    seen with the eyes :
With the half of a broken hope for a pillow at night
That somehow the right is the right
And the smooth shall bloom from the rough :
Lord, if that were enough ?

ROBERT LOUIS STEVENSON

TAKE ME, MOTHER EARTH

TAKE me, Mother Earth, to thy cold breast,
    And fold me there in everlasting rest !
        The long day is o'er;
        I'm weary, I would sleep;
        But deep, deep,
        Never to waken more !

I have had joy and sorrow, I have prov'd
What life could give; have lov'd, and been belov'd;
        I am sick, and heart-sore,
        And weary, let me sleep;
        But deep, deep,
        Never to waken more.

To thy dark chamber, Mother Earth, I come,
Prepare thy dreamless bed in my last home;
        Shut down the marble door,
        And leave me !　Let me sleep;
        But deep, deep,
        Never to waken more !

ANNA JAMESON

THE UNDISCOVERED COUNTRY

COULD we but know
    The land that ends our dark, uncertain travel,
Where lie those happier hills and meadows low,—
Ah, if beyond the 'spirit's inmost cavil,
    Aught of that country could we surely know,
        Who would not go ?

Might we but hear
The hovering angels' high imagined chorus,
    Or catch, betimes, with wakeful eyes and clear,
One radiant vista of the realm before us,—
    With one rapt moment given to see and hear,
        Ah, who would fear ?

Were we quite sure
To find the peerless friend who left us lonely,
    Or there, by some celestial stream as pure,
To gaze in eyes that here were lovelit only,—
    This mortal coil, were we quite sure,
        Who would endure ?

                            EDMUND CLARENCE STEDMAN

See " Hope," a reply to above, in Section Fourth.

SEA-SHELL MURMURS

T HE hollow sea-shell, which for years hath stood
On dusty shelves, when held against the ear
Proclaims its stormy parents ; and we hear
The faint far murmur of the breaking flood.
We hear the sea. The sea ? It is the blood
In our own veins, impetuous and near,
And pulses keeping pace with hope and fear
And with our feelings' every shifting mood.
Lo ! in my heart I hear, as in a shell,
The murmur of a world beyond the grave,
Distinct, distinct, though faint and far it be.
Thou fool ; this echo is a cheat as well,—
The hum of earthly instincts ; and we crave
A world unreal as the shell-heard sea.

EUGENE LEE-HAMILTON

THE SOUL AND THE FUTURE LIFE

If belief be ever permissible—perhaps I ought to
say, if belief be ever possible—on the ground that
"there is peace and joy in believing," it is here, where
the issues are so vast, where the conception in its highest form is so ennobling, where the practical influences
of the Creed are, in appearance, at least, so beneficent.
But faith thus arrived at has ever clinging to it the
curse belonging to all illegitimate possessions. It is
precarious, because the flaw in its title-deeds, barely
suspected perhaps and never acknowledged, may at

any moment be discovered ; misgivings crop up most surely in those hard and gloomy crises of our lives when unflinching confidence is most essential to our peace ; and the fairy fabric, built up not on grounded conviction but on craving need, crumbles into dust, and leaves the spirit with no solid sustenance to rest upon.

Alas ! can the wisest and most sanguine of us all bring anything beyond our own personal sentiments to swell the common hope ? We have aspirations to multiply, but who has any *knowledge* to enrich our store ? I have of course read most of the pleadings in favor of the ordinary doctrine of the future state; naturally also, in common with all graver natures, I have meditated yet more; but these pleadings, for the most part, sound to anxious ears little else than the passionate outcries of souls that cannot endure to part with hopes on which they have been nurtured, and which are intertwined with their tenderest affections. Logical reasons to *compel* conviction, I have met with none. Yet few can have sought for them more yearningly. I may say I share in the anticipations of believers; but I share them as aspirations, sometimes approaching almost to a faith, occasionally, and for a few moments, perhaps rising into something like a trust, but never able to settle into the consistency of a definite and enduring creed. I do not know how far even this incomplete state of mind may not be merely the residuum of early upbringing and habitual associations. But I must be true to my darkness as coura-

geously as to my light. I cannot rest in comfort on
arguments that to my spirit have no cogency, nor can
I pretend to respect or be content with reasons which
carry no penetrating conviction along with them. I
will not make buttresses do the work or assume the
posture of foundations. I will not cry " Peace, peace,
when there is no peace."

The more I think and question, the more do doubts
and difficulties crowd around my horizon, and cloud
over my sky. Thus it is that I am unable to bring
aid or sustainment to minds as troubled as my own,
and perhaps less willing to admit that the great
enigma is, and must remain, insoluble. Of two
things, however, I feel satisfied—that the negative
doctrine is no more susceptible of proof than the
affirmative, and that our opinion, be it only honest, can
have no influence whatever on the issue, nor upon its
bearing on ourselves.

WILLIAM RATHBONE GREG
A modern symposium

OUT OF THE NIGHT

OUT of the night that covers me,
    Black as the pit from pole to pole,
I thank whatever gods may be
    For my unconquerable soul.

In the fell clutch of circumstance
    I have not winced nor cried aloud.
Under the bludgeonings of chance
    My head is bloody, but unbowed.

Prayer

Beyond this place of wrath and tears
   Looms but the horror of the shade,
And yet the menace of the years
   Finds and shall find me unafraid.

It matters not how strait the gate,
   How charged with punishments the scroll,
I am the master of my fate :
   I am the captain of my soul.

WILLIAM ERNEST HENLEY

PRAYER

WHATEVER a man may pray for, he prays for a miracle. Every prayer comes to this : " Great God, let twice two not make four."

Only such a prayer is a real prayer, face to face. To pray to the Spirit of the universe, to the Supreme Being,—to the abstract, unreal god of Kant or Hegel, —is impossible, unthinkable.

But can a personal, living, imaginable God make twice two other than four ?

Every true believer must answer " Yes, He can." And he is obliged to convince himself of it.

But what if his reason rebels against such nonsense ?

Then Shakspere comes to his aid : " There are more things in heaven and earth, Horatio."

But if you seek to controvert him in the name of truth ?—he has merely to repeat the well-known question, " What is truth ? "

And so, let us eat, drink, and be merry,—and pray.

IVAN TURGENEV—Poems in prose

THE WORLD-SOUL

ALAS ! the Sprite that haunts us
 Deceives our rash desire ;
It whispers of the glorious gods,
 And leaves us in the mire.
We cannot learn the cipher
 That's writ upon our cell ;
Stars taunt us by a mystery
 Which we could never spell.

 . . . . .

And what if Trade sow cities
 Like shells along the shore,
And thatch with towns the prairies broad
 With railways ironed o'er ?—
They are but sailing foam-bells
 Along Thought's causing stream,
And take their shape and sun-color
 From him that sends the dream.

 . . . . .

He serveth the servant,
 The brave he loves amain ;
He kills the cripple and the sick,
 And straight begins again ;
For gods delight in gods,
 And thrust the weak aside ;
To him who scorns their charities
 Their arms fly open wide.

RALPH WALDO EMERSON

THE WAYSIDE VIRGIN

I AM the Virgin ; from this granite ledge
   A hundred weary winters I have watched
The lonely road that wanders at my feet,
And many days I've sat here, in my lap
A little heap of snow, and overhead
The dry, dead voices of sere, rustling leaves ;
While scarce a beggar creaked across the way.
How very old I am ; I have forgot
The day they fixed me here ; and whence I came,
With crown of gold, and all my heavenly blue.

How green the grass is now, and all around
Blossoms the May ; but it is cold in here,
Sunless and cold. Now comes a little maid
To kneel among the daisies at my feet ;
What a sweet noise she makes, like murmurings
Of bees in June. I wonder what they say,
These rosy mortals when they look at me ?
I wonder why
They call me Mary, and bow down to me ?
Oh, I am weary of my painted box !
Come child,
And lay thy warm face on my wooden cheek,
That I may feel it glow as once of yore
It glowed when I, a cedar's happy heart,
Felt the first sunshine of the early spring.

UNKNOWN

HONEST DOUBT

YOU say, but with no touch of scorn,
  Sweet-hearted, you, whose light-blue eyes
  Are tender over drowning flies,
You tell me, doubt is Devil-born.

I know not : one indeed I knew
  In many a subtile question versed,
  Who touched a jarring lyre at first,
But ever strove to make it true :

Perplext in faith, but pure in deeds,
  At last he beat his music out.
  There lives more faith in honest doubt,
Believe me, than in half the creeds.

He fought his doubts and gathered strength,
  He would not make his judgment blind,
  He faced the specters of the mind
And laid them : thus he came at length

To find a stronger faith his own ;
  And Power was with him in the night,
  Which makes the darkness and the light,
And dwells not in the light alone,

But in the darkness and the cloud,
  As over Sinai's peaks of old,
  While Israel made their gods of gold,
Altho' the trumpet blew so loud.

37

Why Stand Ye Gazing Into Heaven?

Who loves not knowledge? Who shall rail
   Against her beauty? May she mix
   With men and prosper! Who shall fix
Her pillars? Let her work prevail.

But on her forehead sits a fire:
   She sets her forward countenance
   And leaps into the future chance,
Submitting all things to desire.

Half-grown as yet, a child, and vain—
   She cannot fight the fear of death.
   What is she, cut from love and faith,
But some wild Pallas from the brain

Of Demons? fiery-hot to burst
   All barriers in her onward race
   For power. Let her know her place,
She is the second, not the first.

ALFRED, LORD TENNYSON
In Memoriam

WHY STAND YE GAZING INTO HEAVEN?

WHY stand ye gazing into Heaven?
    What seek ye there? what hope to find
Besides the clouds, which the cold wind
Drives round the world from Morn to Even?
The wan moon, ploughed with ancient scars,
The gracious sun, the alien stars,
    The all-embracing Space?
    Ye look for God?

Why Stand Ye Gazing Into Heaven?

Have ye beheld him there ?
You, or your fathers in their prime ?
Or any man, at any time,
    The wise, the good, the fair ?
Who has beheld—I will not say his face,
        But where his feet have trod ?
    What have your straining eyes
    Discovered in the skies ?
        Why not look down the Sea ?
    'Tis deep, and most creative ; What eludes
    In the upper solitudes,
Still lurking in the lower wastes may be.
Ye look for God, ye tell me.   Tell me this—
        How know ye that He is ?
Because your fathers told ye so, and they
    Because of old, their fathers told them so ;
    As it is now, so was it long ago,
And will be when the years have passed away.

Nothing can come from nothing.   Well, what then ?
The Earth, with all its men,
The little insect burrowing in the sod,
        Sun, planet, star,
        All things that are,
Must have been made by God.
Why made by Him ? Who saw them made ?
Who saw the deep foundations laid ?
        The Hands that built the wall ?
        Why made at all ?
Why not Eternal, tell me ?   Not because

Why Stand Ye Gazing Into Heaven?

It must created be :
If so Eternal He,
But why Eternal ?—why not also This ?
Why must the All be His ?
It was, and is, and is—because it was !

There is no God then ?   Nay,
You say it, and not I ;
I do but say
We have not yet beheld this God on High :
Not knowing that He is, we live and die.
If we know nothing of Him, yet we feel.
We feel love's kisses sweet,
The wine that trips our feet,
The murderous thrust of steel:
Gladness about the heart when the sun breaks,
Or the soft moon is floating up the skies,
Delight in the wild sea, in tranquil lakes,
In every bird that flies ;
And hot tears in our eyes,
When love, the best of earth, its last kiss over—dies !
But He whom we name God, and grope so for above,
Whose arm, we fear, is Power, whose heart, we
hope, is Love
On the worlds below Him,
In the dust before Him,
We may adore Him,
We cannot know Him,
If, indeed, He be, to bless or curse,
And be not this tremendous Universe !

Griefs

"Higher than your arrows fly,
   Deeper than your plummets fall,
Is the Deepest, the Most High,
   Is the All in All!"

RICHARD HENRY STODDARD

GRIEFS

I MEASURE every grief I meet
   With analytic eyes;
I wonder if it weighs like mine,
   Or has an easier size.

I wonder if they bore it long,
   Or did it just begin?
I could not tell the date of mine,
   It feels so old a pain.

I wonder if it hurts to live,
   And if they have to try,
And whether, could they choose between,
   They would not rather die.

I wonder if when years have piled—
   Some thousands—on the cause
Of early hurt, if such a lapse
   Could give them any pause;

Or would they go on aching still
   Through centuries above,
Enlightened to a larger pain
   By contrast with the love.

Losses

The grieved are many, I am told;
  The reason deeper lies—
Death is but one and comes but once,
  And only nails the eyes.

There's grief of want and grief of cold—
  A sort they call " despair ";
There's banishment from native eyes,
  In sight of native air.

And though I may not guess the kind
  Correctly, yet to me
A piercing comfort it affords
  In passing Calvary,

To note the fashions of the cross,
  Of those that stand alone,
Still fascinated to presume
  That some are like my own.

EMILY DICKINSON

LOSSES

UPON the white sea sand
    There sat a pilgrim band,
Telling the losses that their lives had known :
    While evening waned away
    From breezy cliff and bay,
And the strong tides went out with weary moan.

    One spake, with quivering lip,
    Of a fair freighted ship,
With all his household to the deep gone down ;
    But one had wilder woe—

Losses

For a fair face, long ago
Lost in the darker depths of a great town.

There were who mourned their youth
With a most loving ruth,
For its brave hopes and memories ever green ;
And one upon the west
Turned an eye that could not rest,
For far-off hills whereon its joy had been.

Some talked of vanished gold,
Some of proud honors told,
Some spake of friends that were their trust no more ;
And one of a green grave
Beside a foreign wave,
That made him sit so lonely on the shore.

But when their tales were done,
There spake among them one,
A stranger, seeming from all sorrow free :
" Sad losses have ye met,
But mine is heavier yet :
For a believing heart hath gone from me."

" Alas ! " these pilgrims said,
" For the living and the dead—
For fortune's cruelty, for love's sure cross,
For the wrecks of land and sea !
But, however, it came to thee,
Thine, stranger, is life's last and heaviest loss."

FRANCES BROWN

NOT ONE DISSATISFIED

I THINK I could turn and live with animals, they
  are so placid and self-contain'd,
I stand and look at them long and long.
They do not sweat and whine about their condition,
They do not lie awake in the dark and weep for their sins,
They do not make me sick discussing their duty to God,
Not one is dissatisfied, not one is demented with the
  mania of owning things,
Not one kneels to another, nor to his kind that lived
  thousands of years ago,
Not one is respectable or unhappy over the whole
  earth.   WALT WHITMAN

   Song of Myself

WE ARE CHILDREN

CHILDREN indeed are we—children that wait
  Within a wondrous dwelling, while on high
Stretch the sad vapors and the voiceless sky ;
The house is fair, yet all is desolate
Because our Father comes not ; clouds of fate
Sadden above us—shivering we espy
The passing rain, the cloud before the gate,
And cry to one another, " He is nigh ! "
At early morning, with a shining Face,
He left us innocent and lily-crown'd ;
And now this late—night cometh on apace—
We hold each other's hands and look around,
Frighted at our own shades ! Heaven send us grace !
When He returns, all will be sleeping sound.
       ROBERT BUCHANAN

44

DOVER BEACH

THE Sea is calm to-night.
    The tide is full, the moon lies fair
Upon the straits ;—on the French coast the light
Gleams and is gone ; the cliffs of England stand,
Glimmering and vast, out in the tranquil bay.
Come to the window, sweet is the night air !
Only, from the long line of spray
Where the sea meets the moon-blanch'd sand,
Listen !   You hear the grating roar
Of pebbles which the waves draw back, and fling,
At their return, up the high strand,
Begin, and cease, and then again begin,
With tremulous cadence slow, and bring
The eternal note of sadness in.

Sophocles long ago
Heard it on the Ægean, and it brought
Into his mind the turbid ebb and flow
Of human misery ; we
Find also in the sound a thought,
Hearing it by this distant northern sea.

The Sea of faith,
Was once, too, at the full, and round earth's shore
Lay like the folds of a bright girdle furl'd,
But now I only hear
Its melancholy, long, withdrawing roar,
Retreating, to the breath
Of the night-winds, down the vast edges drear
And naked shingles of the world.

On the Shortness of Time

Ah, love, let us be true
To one another ! for the world, which seems
To lie before us like a land of dreams,
So various, so beautiful, so new,
Hath really neither joy, nor love, nor light,
Nor certitude, nor peace, nor help for pain ;
And we are here as on a darkling plain
Swept with confus'd alarms of struggle and flight,
Where ignorant armies clash by night.

MATTHEW ARNOLD

ON THE SHORTNESS OF TIME

IF I could live without the thought of death,
   Forgetful of Time's waste, the soul's decay,
I would not ask for other joy than breath
With light and sound of birds and the sun's ray.
I could sit on untroubled day by day
Watching the grass grow, and the wild flowers range
From blue to yellow and from red to grey
In natural sequence as the seasons change.
I could afford to wait, but for the hurt
Of this dull tick of time which chides my ear.
But now I dare not sit with loins ungirt
And staff unlifted, for death stands too near.
I must be up and doing—ay, each minute.
The grave gives time for rest when we are in it.

WILFRID SCAWEN BLUNT

SOUL AND BODY

WHERE wert thou, Soul, ere yet my body born
    Became thy dwelling-place ? Didst thou on
  earth,
Or in the clouds, await this body's birth ?
Or by what chance upon that winter's morn
Didst thou this body find, a babe forlorn ?
Didst thou in sorrow enter, or in mirth ?
Or for a jest, perchance, to try its worth
Thou tookest flesh, ne'er from it to be torn ?
Nay, Soul, I will not mock thee; well I know
Thou wert not on the earth, nor in the sky;
For with my body's growth thou too didst grow;
But with that body's death wilt thou too die ?
I know not, and thou canst not tell me, so
In doubt we'll go together,—thou and I.

SAMUEL WADDINGTON

THE LOST PLEIAD

GONE, gone !
    O, never more to cheer
The mariner who holds his course alone
On the Atlantic, through the weary night,
When the stars turn to watchers and do sleep,
Shall it appear,
With the sweet fixedness of certain light,
Down-shining on the shut eyes of the deep !

And lone,
Where its first splendors shone,
Shall be that pleasant company of stars :

Siva

How should they know that death
Such perfect beauty mars;
And, like the earth, its common bloom and breath,
Fallen from on high,
Their lights grow blasted by its touch, and die—
All their concerted springs of harmony,
Snapp'd rudely, and the generous music gone.

A strain—a mellow strain—
Of wailing sweetness, fill'd the earth and sky;
The stars lamenting in unborrow'd pain
That one of the selectest ones must die;
Must vanish, when most lovely, from the rest!
Alas! 'tis ever more the destiny,
The hope, the heart-cherish'd, is the soonest lost;
. The flower first budded soonest feels the frost:
Are not the shortest-lived still loveliest?
And like the pale star shooting down the sky,
Look they not ever brightest when they fly
The desolate home they bless'd?

WILLIAM GILMORE SIMMS

SIVA

I AM the God of the sensuous fire
  That molds all Nature in forms divine;
The symbols of death and of man's desire,
  The springs of change in the world, are mine;
The organs of birth and the circlet of bones,
And the light loves carved on the temple stones.

48

Siva

I am the lord of delights and pain,
   Of the pest that killeth, of fruitful joys ;
I rule the currents of heart and vein ;
   A touch gives passion, a look destroys ;
In the heat and cold of my lightest breath
Is the might incarnate of Lust and Death.

If a thousand altars stream with blood
   Of the victims slain by the chanting priest,
Is a great God lured by the savory food ?
   I reck not of worship, or song, or feast ;
But that millions perish, each hour that flies,
Is the mystic sign of my sacrifice.

Ye may plead and pray for the millions born ;
   They come like dew on the morning grass ;
Your vows and vigils I hold in scorn,
   The stage stays never, the stages pass ;
All life is the play of the power that stirs
In the dance of my wanton worshipers.

And the strong, swift river my shrine below
   It runs, like man, its unending course
To the boundless sea from eternal snow ;
   Mine is the Fountain—and mine the Force
That spurs all nature to ceaseless strife ;
And my image is Death at the gates of Life.

In many a legend and many a shape,
   In the solemn grove and the crowded street,
I am the Slayer, whom none escape ;
   I am Death, trod under a fair girl's feet ;

Siva

I govern the tides of the sentient sea
That ebbs and flows to eternity.

And the sum of the thought and the knowledge of man
   Is the secret tale that my emblems tell ;
Do you seek God's purpose, or trace his plan ?
   Ye may read your doom in my parable :
For the circle of life in its flower and fall
Is the writing that runs on my temple wall.

O race that labors, and seeks, and strives,
   With thy Faith, thy wisdom, thy hopes and fears,
Where now is the Future of myriad lives ?
   Where now is the creed of a thousand years ?
Far as the Western spirit may range,
It finds but the travail of endless change.

For the earth is fashioned by countless suns,
   And planets wander, and stars are lost,
As the rolling flood of existence runs
   From light to shadow, from fire to frost.
Your search is ended, ye hold the keys
Of my inmost ancient mysteries.

Now that your hands have lifted the veil,
   And the crowd may know what my symbols mean,
Will not the faces of men turn pale
   At the sentence heard, and the vision seen
Of strife and sleep, of the soul's brief hour,
And the careless tread of unyielding Power ?

Though the world repent of its cruel youth,
   And in age grow soft, and its hard law bend,

When We Are All Asleep

Ye may spare or slaughter ; by rage or ruth
  All forms speed on to the still far end ;
For the gods who have mercy, who save or bless,
Are the visions of man in his hopefulness.

Let my temples fall, they are dark with age ;
  Let my idols break, they have stood their day ;
On their deep hewn stones the primeval sage
  Has figured the spells that endure alway ;
My presence may vanish from river and grove,
But I rule forever in Death and Love.

SIR ALFRED LYALL

WHEN WE ARE ALL ASLEEP

WHEN He returns, and finds the world so drear,
    All sleeping, young and old, unfair and fair,
Will He stoop down and whisper in each ear,
" Awaken ! " or for pity's sake forbear,
Saying, " How shall I meet their frozen stare
Of wonder, and their eyes so full of fear ?
How shall I comfort them in their despair,
If they cry out ' Too late, let us sleep here ' ? "
Perchance He will not wake us up, but when
He sees us look so happy in our rest,
Will murmur, " Poor dead women and dead men !
Dire was their doom, and weary was their quest.
Wherefore wake them into life again ?
Let them sleep on untroubled—it is best."

ROBERT BUCHANAN

DE mortuis nil nisi bonum.   When
    For me the end has come and I am dead,
And little, voluble, chattering daws of men
    Peck at me curiously, let it then be said
By some one brave enough to speak the truth,
    Here lies a great soul killed by cruel wrong.
Down all the balmy days of his fresh youth
    To his bleak, desolate noon, with sword and song,
And speech that rushed up hotly from the heart,
    He wrought for liberty ; till his own wound,
(He had been stabbed) concealed with painful art
    Through wasting years, mastered him and he
      swooned,
And sank there where you see him lying now,
With that word Failure written on his brow.

But say that he succeeded.   If he missed
    World's honors and world's plaudits, and the wage
Of the world's deft lackeys, still his lips were kissed
    Daily by those high angels who assuage
The thirstings of the poets—for he was
    Born unto singing—and a burden lay
Mightily on him, and he moaned because
    He could not rightly utter to his day
What God taught in the night.   Sometimes, natheless
    Power fell upon him, and bright tongues of flame
And blessings reached him from poor souls in stress ;
    And benedictions from black pits of shame ;
And little children's love ; and old men's prayers ;
And a Great Hand that led him unawares.

De Mortuis Nil Nisi Bonum

So he died rich.   And if his eyes were blurred
  With thick films—silence, for he is in his grave.
Greatly he suffered ; greatly, too, he erred ;
  Yet broke his heart in trying to be brave.
Nor did he wait till Freedom had become
  The popular shibboleth of courtiers' lips ;
But smote for her when God himself seemed dumb,
  And all his arching skies were in eclipse ;
He was aweary, but he fought his fight,
  And stood for simple manhood ; and was joyed
To see the august broadening of the light,
  And new earths heaving heavenward from the void.
He loved his fellows, and their love was sweet—
Plant daisies at his head and at his feet.

RICHARD REALF

Rossiter Johnson, in LIPPINCOTT'S MAGAZINE, March, 1879:
Richard Realf was an English peasant, born near Brighton, Sussex,
in 1834. As a boy his poetic talents attracted the interest of Lady
Byron and Rev. Frederick W. Robertson. He came to New York in
1854; in 1862 he enlisted in the Northern Army; at the close of the
war he became a journalist. His career was now one of bitter misfortune; his poems, thrown off as mere incidents in his newspaper
work, have never been collected and published. They evince rare
powers of thought, feeling, and expression. Richard Realf died, by his
own hand, in San Francisco, in 1878, having just written the lines,
" De mortuis nil nisi bonum."

BEFORE the beginning of years
  There came to the making of man
Time, with a gift of tears ;
  Grief, with a glass that ran ;
Pleasure, with sin for leaven ;
  Summer, with flowers that fell ;
Remembrance, fallen from heaven ;
  And madness, risen from hell ;
Strength, without hands to smite ;
  Love, that endures for a breath ;
Night, the shadow of light ;
  And life, the shadow of death.

And the high gods took in hand
  Fire and the falling of tears,
And a measure of sliding sand
  From under the feet of the years,
And froth and drift of the sea,
  And dust of the laboring earth,
And bodies of things to be
  In the houses of death and of birth,
And wrought with weeping and laughter,
  And fashioned with loathing and love,
With life before and after,
  And death beneath and above,
For a night and a day and a morrow,
  That his strength might endure for a span,
With travail and heavy sorrow,
  The holy spirit of man.

Bubbles

From the winds of the North and the South
  They gathered us unto strife ;
They breathed up in his mouth,
  They filled his body with life ;
Eyesight and speech they wrought
  For the veils of the soul therein ·
A time for labor and thought,
  A time to serve and to sin ;
They gave him light in his ways,
  And love, and a space for delight,
And beauty and length of days,
  And night, and sleep in the night.
His speech is a burning fire ;
  With his lips he travaileth ;
In his heart is a blind desire,
  In his eyes foreknowledge of death.
He weaves, and is clothed in derision ;
  Sows, and he shall not reap ;
His life is a watch or a vision
  Between a sleep and a sleep.

ALGERNON CHARLES SWINBURNE

BUBBLES

I

I STOOD on the brink in childhood,
  And watched the bubbles go
From the rock-fretted, sunny ripple
  To the smoother tide below ;

Bubbles

And over the white creek bottom,
  Under them every one,
Went golden stars in the water,
  All luminous with the sun.

But the bubbles broke on the surface;
  And under, the stars of gold
Broke; and the hurrying water
  Flowed onward, swift and cold.

II

I stood on the brink in manhood,
  And it came to my weary brain,
And my heart, so dull and heavy
  After the years of pain,—

That every hollowest bubble
  Which over my life had passed
Still into its deeper current
  Some heavenly gleam had cast;

That however I mocked it gayly,
  And guessed at its hollowness,
Still shone, with each bursting bubble,
  One star in my soul the less.

WILLIAM DEAN HOWELLS

THE MIRAGE

I SEE a city fair and bright,
  With glittering dome and lofty tower,
As gliding onward through the night
  We tell the lonely midnight hour.

I seem to see a busy throng
  Upon its dimly outlined shore ;
I listen for a burst of song—
  I hark for plash of falling oar,

In vain !   Eternal silence swings
  Around that city's gleaming walls,
Within it is no voice that sings,
  From out its port no echo falls.

We draw no nearer to its gate,
  We enter not those portals fair,
For as the hour grows chill and late
  It vanishes into the air !

Oh, Phantom City of the Plain,
  Whose mocking lights illusive gleam,
Our lives are spent in quest as vain,
  We wake, and lo, 'twas all a dream !

VOLNEY STREAMER

Southern Pacific Railway, November 18, 1888.

DOUBT

'TIS nature's law: that once at rest,
    The boulder should forever lie
Unmoved beneath the placid sky,
Asleep upon earth's quiet breast;

That once in motion, worlds shall sweep
    Forever on their destined way;
    That, through the night and through the day,
Unswerved their pathways they should keep.

And so the mind of man would cling
    Forever to its old-time faith,
    Whatever word the new age saith,
Whatever light the new suns bring.

Unquiet are the waves of doubt
    That toss forever round the world,
    On which our restless ships are whirled
As tides flow in and tides flow out.

But rotting on the oozy strands,
    Our ships would crumble and decay,
    Did not the waves about them play,
And sweep them off to other lands.

MINOT JUDSON SAVAGE

The same day came to him the Sadducees, which say there is no resurrection.—St. Matthew, xxii, 23.

PRIMITIVE man saw the reflection of his face in streams or crystals; he heard the echo of his voice returned from cliffs; he dreamed dreams into which the living and the dead came and went without distinction; little wonder that he began to believe in "doubles," that he imagined himself to be possessed of a "soul," separable from his body and surviving his body's death. Nor were moral feelings wanting in support of his faith. Many a good man's life was miserable ; many another life, happy enough, was abruptly ended at its very dawn. Surely, he thought, there must be another state of being to redress the wrongs and hardships of this.

But with advancing knowledge the old faith retires. Immanence is the key-thought of modern philosophy. Man is no longer regarded as two beings, but as one. Nature is viewed as moving by inherent, not external forces : the attempt to account for Nature by Supernature is detected as verbal merely—no genuine thought standing behind the words. It is felt that whatever may be the link between mind and body, if indeed they be not twin manifestations of the same thing, nothing is gained by positing a "spirit" in explanation.

The ancient faith in the immortal "soul" is undermined by the progress of knowledge at other points.

A Sadducee's View

Man has learned to parry the evil forces of nature; pain is abolished by anesthetics; disease is not simply ousted by scores of new weapons, it is in many cases absolutely denied any foothold whatever. Thanks, also, to new knowledge, positive pleasures abound and superabound where of old they were unknown and unimagined. Comforts, luxuries, ministries to the best tastes and highest feelings, are fast passing from the few to the whole body of the people. Man is to-day the master of his fate as never before. Life lengthens at the same time that it becomes better worth having while it lasts. When one sees a youth cut off on the very threshold of his career, there is a suggestion that the broken arc of his life may be prolonged in another state of being. But when one sees an old man who has lived according to knowledge, with faculties fading as gradually as they awakened eighty or ninety years before, one is looking not at a broken arc, but at a full circle—whose completed round has no suggestion of aught beyond the grave. It is this old man, not the youth prematurely cut off, who is the type of the coming man—who will rejoice that he was born, who, happy and contented, partly by virtue of the moral struggle which will always remain, will need no " consolations " and ask none, resigning Great Expectations of life beyond the stars as proper only to the childhood of the race. He will need no Faith, he will See : he will lean on no Hope, he will Have.

UNKNOWN.

60

FAITH

THERE is a startling legend that is known
　　　To Spanish scholars : how the fertile land
　For years was ravaged by a robber band,
Led by a knight with visor ever down ;

And how, at last, when he was overthrown,
　　The shape which made so desperate a stand
　　And quivered still, was found to be, when scann'd,
A suit of armor, empty heel to crown.

Naught fights like Emptiness.　Beneath the veil
　Of Islam's warlike Prophet, from Bagdad
To Roncevaux, it made the nations quail;

And once, as Templar and Crusader clad,
　It shook the world.　Ev'n now, Faith's empty mail
Still writhes and struggles with the life it had.

EUGENE LEE-HAMILTON

A RECUSANT

THE Church stands there beyond the orchard-
　　　　blooms;
　How yearningly I gaze upon its spire !
Lifted mysterious through the twilight glooms,
　Dissolving in the sunset's golden fire,
Or dim as slender incense morn by morn
　Ascending to the blue and open sky.

Beyond

Forever when my heart feels most forlorn
 It murmurs to me with a weary sigh,
How sweet to enter in, to kneel and pray
 With all the others whom we love so well !
All disbelief and doubt might pass away,
 All peace float to us with its Sabbath bell.
Conscience replies, There is but one good rest,
Whose head is pillowed upon Truth's pure breast.

JAMES THOMSON

BEYOND

THERE'S a fancy some lean to and others hate—
 That, when this life is ended begins
New work for the soul in another state,
 Where it strives and gets weary, loses and wins ;
Where the strong and the weak, this world's congeries,
 Repeat in large what they practiced in small,
Through life after life in unlimited series ;
 Only the scale's to be changed, that's all.

Yet I hardly know. When a soul has seen
 By the means of Evil that Good is best,
And, through earth and its noise, what is heaven's
  serene—
 When our faith in the same has stood the test—
Why, the child grown man, you burn the rod,
 The uses of labor are surely done ;
There remaineth a rest for the people of God :
 And I have had troubles enough, for one.

ROBERT BROWNING

Light on the Cloud

There is nothing either good or bad,
But thinking makes it so.

SHAKSPERE

He that planted the ear, shall he not hear?
He that formed the eye, shall he not see?
He that teacheth man knowledge, shall he not know?

PSALM XCIV

To hope and not to be impatient is really to believe.

GEORGE MEREDITH

DOUBT

THEY bade me cast the thing away,
　　They pointed to my hands all bleeding,
They listened not to all my pleading ;
　The thing I meant I could not say :
　I knew that I should rue the day
　If once I cast that thing away.

　I grasped it firm, and bore the pain ;
The thorny husks I stripped and scattered ;
If I could reach its heart, what mattered
　If other men saw not my gain,
　Or even if I should be slain ?
　I knew the risks ; I chose the pain.

　Oh, had I cast that thing away,
I had not found what most I cherish,
A faith without which I should perish,
　The faith which, like a kernel, lay
　Hid in the husks which on that day
　My instinct would not throw away !

HELEN HUNT JACKSON

We read the pagans' sacred books with profit and delight. With myth and fable we are ever charmed, and find a pleasure in the endless repetition of the beautiful, poetic, and absurd. We find, in all these records of the past, philosophies and dreams, and efforts stained with tears of great and tender souls, who tried to pierce the mystery of life and death, to answer the eternal questions of the Whence and Whither, and vainly sought to make, with bits of shattered glass, a mirror that would in every breath reflect the face and form of Nature's perfect self.

These myths were born of hopes, and fears, and tears, and smiles, and they were touched and colored by all there is of joy and grief between the rosy dawn of birth and death's sad night. They clothed even the stars with passion, and gave to gods the virtues, faults, and frailties of the sons of men. In them, the winds and waves were music, and all the lakes, and streams, and springs—the mountains, woods, and per-fumed dells, were haunted by a thousand fairy forms. They thrilled the veins of Spring with tremulous desire ; made tawny Summer's billowed breast the throne and home of love ; filled Autumn's arms with sun-kissed grapes and gathered sheaves; and pictured Winter as a weak old king, who felt, like Lear, upon his withered face, Cordelia's tears. These myths, though false, are beautiful, and have for many ages, and in countless ways, enriched the heart, and kindled thought. But if the world were taught that all these things are true, and all inspired of God, and that eternal punishment will be the lot of him who dares deny or doubt, the sweetest myth of all the Fable-World will lose its beauty and become a scorned and hateful thing to every brave and thoughtful man.

ROBERT G. INGERSOLL

Prose Poems

Copyright 1884, by C. P. Farrell

THE PANTHEIST'S SONG OF IMMORTALITY

BRING snow-white lilies, pallid heart-flushed roses,
   Enwreathe her brow with heavy scented flowers;
In soft undreaming sleep her head reposes,
   While, unregretted, pass the sunlit hours.

Few sorrows did she know—and all are over ;
   A thousand joys—but they are all forgot ;
Her life was one fair dream of friend and lover,
   And were they false—ah well, she knows it not.

Look in her face and lose thy dread of dying ;
   Weep not that rest will come, that toil will cease ;
Is it not well to lie as she is lying,
   In utter silence, and in perfect peace ?

Canst thou repine that sentient days are numbered ?
   Death is unconscious Life, that waits for birth ;
So didst thou live, while yet thine embryo slumbered,
   Senseless, unbreathing, even as heaven and earth.

The Pantheist's Song of Immortality

Then shrink no more from Death, though Life be glad-
    ness,
  Nor seek him, restless in thy lonely pain ;
The law of joy ordains each hour of sadness,
  And firm or frail, thou canst not live in vain.

What though thy name by no sad lips be spoken,
  And no fond heart shall keep thy memory green ?
Thou yet shalt leave thine own enduring token,
  For earth is not as though thou ne'er hadst been.

See yon broad current, hasting to the ocean,
  Its ripples glorious in the western red :
Each wavelet passes, trackless ; yet its motion
  Has changed for evermore the river bed.

Ah, wherefore weep, although the form and fashion
  Of what thou seemest fades like sunset flame ?
The uncreated Source of toil and passion
  Through everlasting change abides the same.

Yes, thou shalt die ; but these almighty forces,
  That meet to form thee, live for evermore ;
They hold the suns in their eternal courses,
  And shape the tiny sand-grains on the shore.

Be calmly glad, thine own true kindred seeing
  In fire and storm, in flowers with dew impearled ;
Rejoice in thine imperishable being,
  One with the essence of the boundless world.

          CONSTANCE CAROLINE WOODHILL NADEN

THE BEAUTIFUL CITY

THE Beautiful City ! forever
    Its rapturous praises resound ;
We fain would behold it—but never
    A glimpse of its glory is found :
We slacken our lips at the tender
    White breasts of our mothers to hear
Of its marvelous beauty and splendor ;—
    We see—but the gleam of a tear !

Yet never the story may tire us—
    First graven on symbols of stone—
Rewritten on scrolls of papyrus,
    And parchment, and scattered and blown
By the winds of the tongues of all Nations,
    Like a litter of leaves wildly whirled
Down the rack of a hundred translations,
    From the earliest lisp of the world.

We compass the earth and the ocean,
    From the Orient's uttermost light,
To where the last ripple of motion
    Lips hem of the skirt of the night,—
But The Beautiful City evades us—
    No spire of it glints in the sun—
No glad-bannered battlement shades us
    When all our long journey is done.

The Beautiful City

Where lies it ?   We question and listen ;
  We lean from the mountain, or mast,
And see but dull earth, or the glisten
  Of seas inconceivably vast ;
The dust of the one blurs our vision—
  The glare of the other our brain,
Nor city nor island elysian
  In all of the land or the main !

We kneel in dim fanes where the thunders
  Of organs tumultuous roll,
And the longing heart listens and wonders,
  And the eyes look aloft from the soul,
But the chanson grows fainter and fainter,
  Swoons wholly away and is dead ;
And our eyes only reach where the painter
  Has dabbled a saint overhead.

The Beautiful City !   O Mortal,
  Fare hopefully on in thy quest,
Pass down through the green grassy portal
  That leads to the Valley of Rest,
There first passed the One who, in pity
  Of all thy great yearning, awaits
To point out The Beautiful City,
  And loosen the trump at the gates.

JAMES WHITCOMB RILEY

THE wish that of the living whole
    No life may fail beyond the grave,
    Derives it not from what we have
The likest God within the soul ?

Are God and Nature then at strife,
    That Nature lends such evil dreams ?
    So careful of the type she seems,
So careless of the single life ;

That I, considering everywhere
    Her secret meaning in her deeds,
    And finding that of fifty seeds
She often brings but one to bear,

I falter where I firmly trod,
    And falling with my weight of cares
    Upon the great world's altar-stairs
That slope through darkness up to God,

I stretch lame hands of faith, and grope,
    And gather dust and chaff, and call
    To what I feel is Lord of all,
And faintly trust the larger hope.

" So careful of the type ? " But no.
    From scarped cliff and quarried stone
    She cries, " A thousand types are gone :
I care for nothing, all shall go.

Behind the Veil

" Thou makest thine appeal to me :
     I bring to life, i bring to death :
     The spirit does but mean the breath :
I know no more."   And he, shall he,

Man, her last work, who seem'd so fair,
     Such splendid purpose in his eyes,
     Who roll'd the psalm to wintry skies,
Who built him fanes of fruitless prayer,

Who trusted God was love indeed
     And love Creation's final law,—
     Tho' Nature, red in tooth and claw
With ravine, shriek'd against his creed,—

Who loved, who suffer'd countless ills,
     Who battled for the True, the Just,
     Be blown about the desert dust,
Or seal'd within the iron hills ?

No more ?   A monster then, a dream,
     A discord.   Dragons of the prime,
     That tear each other in their slime,
Were mellow music matched with him.

O life as futile, then, as frail !
     O for thy voice to soothe and bless !
     What hope of answer, or redress ?
Behind the veil, behind the veil.

                    ALFRED, LORD TENNYSON
                         In Memoriam

OPTIMISM AND PESSIMISM

I ASSURE you in all earnestness, speaking as an idealist, as one who longs to have men recognize the spiritual order, to believe in the supremacy of the good in this our world, to rise above sense, and to feel secure of the rationality of the universe,—speaking thus, I still regard as one of the most lamentable and disheartening features in our modern life the dreary opposition between those who, studying the order of nature as science shows it, remain agnostic about the spiritual realities of the world, and those who, on the other hand, believing, as they say, in a divine order, remain gently optimistic, and refuse to look at the woes and horrors of the world of Darwin and science, because forsooth, since the Lord reigns, all must be right with the world. Thus on the one hand we have a romantic idealism that loves with false liberalism, to cheapen religious faith by ignoring all the graver dogmas of the traditional creeds, that invents meanwhile social utopias, that denies the profound waywardness and wickedness of human nature, and that refuses to grapple by the throat the real evils of life; while on the other hand we have an agnosticism that refuses to believe in the spiritual, because once for all there is so much mischief in the phenomenal order of nature. A genuine synthesis of this optimism and its opposing pessimism, a spiritual idealism that does not deny the reality and the gravity of evil, a religion that looks forward to the day of the Lord as to something very great and therefore very serious, and that accepts life as something valuable enough to be tragic —this is what we need. JOSIAH ROYCE

The spirit of modern philosophy

THE SPECTRUM

HOW many colors do we see set,
    Like rings upon God's finger? Some say three,
Some four, some six, some seven.   All agree
To left of red, to right of violet,
Waits darkness deep as night and black as jet.
And so we know what Noah saw we see,
Nor less nor more—of God's emblazonry
A shred—a sign of glory known not yet.
If red can glide to yellow, green to blue,
What joys may yet await our wider eyes
When we rewake upon a wider shore!
What deep pulsations exquisite and new!
What keener, swifter raptures may surprise
Men born to see the rainbow and no more!

COSMO MONKHOUSE

THERE IS A WOUND WITHIN ME

THERE is a wound within me, 'tis a wound
    That lies too deep for tears, and many a while,
While that is around me seems to smile,
Within my heart of hearts a knell doth sound,
Not of this world ; a cloud dark and profound
Is o'er me, and though brighter thoughts beguile,
And, like the sun, behind a cloudy pile,
Bright gleams from One beyond that cloud have bound,
Yet 'tis a cloud, for I have pierced deep
The side of One that must be All in All.
In this dread calm, if unto Thee I call,
'Tis not that Thou my wounded soul wouldst steep
With aught of gladness ; but that I, through Thee,
May daily put me on more deep humility.

ISAAC WILLIAMS
The Golden Valley

HUMAN BETTERMENT

THAT man, as a "political animal," is susceptible
    of a vast amount of improvement, by education,
by instruction, and by the application of his intelligence
to the adaptation of the conditions of life to his higher
needs, 1 entertain not the slightest doubt. But, so long
as he remains liable to error, intellectual or moral ; so
long as he is compelled to be perpetually on guard against
the cosmic forces, whose ends are not his ends, without
and within himself ; so long as he is haunted by inex-
pugnable memories and hopeless aspirations ; as long

Brahma

as the recognition of his intellectual limitations forces
him to acknowledge his incapacity to penetrate the mystery of existence ; the prospect of attaining untroubled
happiness, or of a state which can, even remotely, de-
serve the title of perfection, appears to me as misleading an illusion as ever was dangled before the eyes of
poor humanity.   And there have been many of them.

That which lies before the human race is a constant
struggle to maintain and improve, in opposition to a State
of Nature, the State of Art of an organized polity ; in
which, and by which, man may develop a worthy civilization, capable of maintaining and constantly improv-
ing itself, until the evolution of our globe shall have
entered so far upon its downward course that the
cosmic process resumes its sway ; and, once more, the
State of Nature prevails over the surface of our planet.

THOMAS HENRY HUXLEY
Evolution and Ethics

BRAHMA

IF the red slayer thinks he slays,
  Or if the slain thinks he is slain,
They know not well the subtle ways
  I keep, and pass, and turn again.

Far or forgot to me is near,
  Shadow and sunlight are the same ;
The vanished gods to me appear,
  And one to me are shame and fame.

Awakening

They reckon ill who leave me out.
    When me they fly, I am the wings ;
I am the doubter and the doubt,
    And I the hymn the Brahman sings.

The strong gods pine for my abode,
    And pine in vain the sacred seven ;
But thou, meek lover of the good,
    Find me, and turn thy back on heaven.

RALPH WALDO EMERSON

AWAKENING

WITH brain o'erworn, with heart a summer clod,
    With eye so practiced in each form around,—
And all forms mean,—to glance above the ground
Irks it, each day of many days we plod,
Tongue-tied and deaf, along life's common road ;
    But suddenly, we know not how, a sound
    Of living streams, an odor, a flower crowned
With dew, a lark upspringing from the sod,
And we awake. O joy of deep amaze !
    Beneath the everlasting hills we stand,
    We hear the voices of the morning seas,
    And earnest prophesyings in the land,
While from the open heaven leans forth at gaze
    The encompassing great cloud of witnesses.

EDWARD DOWDEN

THE CIRCUIT OF BEING

THE snowflake that glistens at morn on Kailasa,
  Dissolved by the sunbeams, descends to the
    plain;
Then, mingling with Gunga, it floats to the ocean,
  And lost in its waters returns not again.

On the roseleaf at sunrise bright glistens the dewdrop
  That in vapor exhaled falls in nourishing rain;
Then in rills back to Gunga through green fields
    meanders,
  Till onward it flows to the ocean again.

A snowflake still whitens the peak of Kailasa,
  But the snowflake of yesterday flows to the main;
At dawning a dewdrop still hangs on the roseleaf,
  But the dewdrop of yesterday comes not again.

The soul that is freed from the bondage of nature
  Escapes from illusions of joy and of pain;
And, pure as the flame that is lost in the sunbeams,
  Ascends unto God, and returns not again.
It comes not and goes not, it comes not again.

UNKNOWN

Credited to a missionary in Northern India

SUPERSTITION IS PRIMITIVE SCIENCE

WHEN people like the American Indians or the
  African negroes believe that the air around
them is swarming with invisible spirits, this is not non-

sense. They mean that life is full of accidents which do not happen of themselves; and when in their rude philosophy they say the spirits make them happen, this is finding the most distinct causes which their minds can understand.

We know how strong our own desire is to account for everything. The desire is as strong among barbarians, and accordingly they devise such explanations as satisfy their minds. But they are apt to go a stage further, and their explanations turn into the form of stories with names of places and persons, thus becoming full-made myths. Educated men do not now consider it honest to make fictitious history in this way, but people of untrained mind, in what is called the myth-making stage, which has lasted on from the savage period, and has not quite disappeared among ourselves, have no such scruples about converting their guesses at what may have happened, into the most lifelike stories of what they say did happen.

The notion of soul or spirit helped men on to the notion of cause. When the cause of anything presents itself to the ancient mind as a kind of soul or spirit, then the cause or spirit of summer, sleep, hope, justice, comes easily to look like a person.

The African or Hindu explains that he believes a stock or stone to be a receptacle in which a divine spirit has for a time embodied itself.

EDWARD B. TYLOR

Anthropology

PROSPICE

FEAR death ? to feel the fog in my throat,
>   The mist in my face,
When the snows begin, and the blasts denote
>   I am nearing the place,
The power of the night, the press of the storm,
>   The post of the foe ;
Where he stands, the Arch Fear, in a visible form,
>   Yet the strong man must go,
For the journey is done and the summit attain'd,
>   And the barriers fall,
Though a battle's to fight ere the guerdon be gain'd,
>   The reward of it all.
I was ever a fighter, so——one fight more,
>   The best and the last !
I would hate that death bandaged my eyes, and forbore
>   And bade me creep past.
No ! let me taste the whole of it, fare like my peers
>   The heroes of old,
Bear the brunt, in a minute pay glad life's arrears
>   Of pain, darkness, and cold.
For sudden the worst turns the best to the brave,
>   The black minute's at end,
And the elements' rage, the fiend-voices that rave,
>   Shall dwindle, shall blend,
Shall change, shall become first a peace out of pain.
>   Then a light, then thy breast,
O thou soul of my soul ! I shall clasp thee again,
>   And with God be the rest.

ROBERT BROWNING

OUR SHARE OF NIGHT TO BEAR

OUR share of night to bear,
    Our share of morning,
Our blank in bliss to fill,
    Our blank in scorning.

Here a star, and there a star,
    Some lose their way.
Here a mist, and there a mist,
    Afterwards—day !

EMILY DICKINSON

EXPLANATION, NOT ATTACK

NO one of any sense or knowledge now thinks the Christian religion had its origin in deliberate imposture. The modern freethinker does not attack it, he explains it. And what is more, he explains it by referring its growth to the better, and not to the worse, part of human nature. He traces it to men's cravings for a higher morality. He finds its source in their aspirations after nobler expression of that feeling for the incommensurable things, which is in truth under so many varieties of inwoven pattern the common universal web of religious faith.

JOHN MORLEY
On Compromise

THE IMMORTAL MIND

WHEN coldness wraps this suffering clay,
  Ah, whither strays the immortal mind?
It cannot die, it cannot stay,
  But leaves its darkened dust behind,
Then, unembodied, doth it trace
  By steps each planet's heavenly way?
Or fill at once the realms of space,
  A thing of eyes, that all survey?

Eternal, boundless, undecayed,
  A thought unseen, but seeing all,
All, all in earth or skies displayed,
  Shall it survey, shall it recall;
Each fainter trace that memory holds
  So darkly of departed years,
In one broad glance the soul beholds,
  And all that was at once appears.

Before creation peopled earth,
  Its eyes shall roll through chaos back;
And where the farthest heaven had birth,
  The spirit trace its rising track,
And where the future mars or makes,
  Its glance dilate o'er all to be,
While sun is quenched or system breaks,
  Fixed in its own eternity.

The Rise of the Doctrine of Evolution

Above or love, hope, hate, or fear,
    It lives all passionless and pure :
An age shall fleet like earthly year ;
    Its years as moments shall endure.
Away, away, without a wing,
    O'er all, through all, its thoughts shall fly,—
A nameless and eternal thing,
    Forgetting what it was to die.

            GEORGE GORDON, LORD BYRON

THE RISE OF THE DOCTRINE OF EVOLUTION

OUR language, our institutions, our beliefs, our ideals, whatever, in short, is mightiest and dearest in all our world, all this together is a slow and hard-won growth, nobody's arbitrary invention, no gift from above, no outcome of a social compact, no immediate expression of reason, but the slowly formed concretion of ages of blind effort, unconscious, but wise in its unconsciousness, often selfish, but humane even in its selfishness. The ideals win the battle of life by the secret connivance, as it were, of numberless seemingly un-ideal forces. Climate, hunger, commerce, authority, superstition, war, cruelty, toil, greed, compromise, tradition, conservatism, loyalty, sloth,—all these coöperate, through countless ages, with a hundred other discernible tendencies, to build up civilization. And civilization itself is, in consequence, a much deeper thing than appears on the surface of the consciousness.

The Rise of the Doctrine of Evolution

Instinct has a larger share in it than reasoning. Faith counts for more in it than insight. It embodies in concrete form that deeper self that the idealists loved to talk about. Your deeper self is plainly a sort of abstract and epitome of the whole history of humanity. A new and wiser form of the doctrine of metempsychosis occurs to you. The humanity that toiled and bled and worshiped of old has transmitted to you, in your language and institutions, in the ancient lore that your fathers teach you, in your prejudices, in your faults, in your conscience, in your religion, the very soul of its agony and of its glory. You can read in history your personal instincts written in the language of evolution. You can watch the human spirit in its growth with a deeper sense of the " That art Thou " than you had ever before possessed. The metaphors of your heathen ancestors are crystallized in every word that you utter. The very horrors of their superstitions are the true though humble origin of your loftiest and most sacred devotions. Humanity never really forsakes its past. The days of mankind are bound each to each in mutual piety.

JOSIAH ROYCE

The spirit of modern philosophy

LIKE ONE WHO WALKETH IN A PLENTE-
OUS LAND

LIKE one who walketh in a plenteous land,
　　By flowing waters, under shady trees,
Through sunny meadows, where the summer bees
Feed in the thyme and clover ; on each hand
Fair gardens lying, where of fruit and flower
The bounteous season hath poured out its dower :
Where saffron skies roof in the earth with light,
And birds sing thankfully toward Heaven, while he
With a sad heart walks through this jubilee,
Beholding how beyond this happy land,
Stretches a thirsty desert of gray sand,
Where all the air is one thick, leaden blight,
Where all things dwarf and dwindle,—so walk I,
Through my rich, present life, to what beyond doth lie.

FRANCES ANNE KEMBLE

LIFE

LIFE ! I know not what thou art,
　　But know that thou and I must part ;
And when, or how, or where we met,
I own to me's a secret yet.
But this I know : when thou art fled,
Where'er they lay these limbs, this head,
No clod so valueless shall be
As all that then remains of me.

85

Life

Oh, whither, whither dost thou fly,
Where bend unseen thy trackless course,
And in this strange divorce,
Ah, tell me where I must seek this compound I ?

To the vast ocean of empyreal flame,
From whence thy essence came,
Dost thou thy flight pursue, when freed
From matter's base encumbering weed ?
Or dost thou, hid from sight,
Wait like some spell-bound knight,
Through blank oblivious years the appointed hour
To break thy trance and reassume thy power ?
Yet canst thou without thought or feeling be ?
Oh, say, what art thou, when no more thou'rt thee ?
Life ! We've been long together
Through pleasant and through cloudy weather ;
'Tis hard to part when friends are dear ;
Perhaps 'twill cost a sigh, a tear ;
Then steal away, give little warning,
Choose thine own time ;
Say not Good-night—but in some brighter clime
Bid me Good-morning.

ANNA LETITIA BARBAULD

" ART thou in love with men's praises, get thee into the very soul of them, and see !—what judges they be, even in those matters which concern themselves. Wouldst thou have their praises after death, bethink thee, that they who shall come hereafter, and with whom thou wouldst survive by thy great name, will be but as these, whom here thou hast found so hard to live with. For, of a truth, his soul who is aflutter upon renown after death, presents not this aright to itself, that of all whose memory he would have, each one will likewise quickly depart, until memory herself be put out, as she journeys on by means of such as are themselves on the wing but for a while, and are extinguished in their turn. Making so much of those thou wilt never see ! It is as if thou wouldst have had those who were before thee discourse fair things concerning thee.

"To him, indeed, whose wit hath been whetted by true doctrine, that well-worn sentence of Homer sufficeth, to guard him against regret and fear.

Like the race of leaves
The race of man is :—
The wind in autumn strows
The earth with old leaves: then the spring the woods
with new endows—

Leaves ! little leaves !—thy children, thy flatterers, thine enemies ! Leaves in the wind, those who would devote thee to darkness, who scorn or miscall thee here, even as they also whose great fame shall outlast them. For all these, and the like of them, are born indeed in the spring season—and soon a wind hath scattered them, and thereafter the wood peopleth itself again with another generation of leaves. And what is common to all of them is but the littleness of their lives : and yet wouldst thou love and hate, as if these things should continue for ever. In a little while thine eyes also will be closed, and he on whom thou perchance hast leaned thyself be himself a burden upon another."

WALTER PATER
Marius the Epicurean

PROGRESS

INSECT and reptile, fish and bird and beast,
   Cast their worn robes aside fresh robes to don ;
Tree, flower, and moss, put new year's raiment on ;
Each natural type, the greatest as the least,
Renews its vesture when the use hath ceased.
   How should man's spirit keep in unison
   With the world's law of outgrowth, save it won
New robes and ampler as its girth increased ?
Quit shrunken creed, and dwarfed philosophy !
   Let gently die an art's decaying fire !
Work on the ancient lines, but yet be free
   To leave and frame anew, if God inspire !
The planets change their surface as they roll :
The force that binds the spheres must bind the soul.

HENRY G. HEWLETT

THE SPIDER

A NOISELESS patient spider,
   I mark'd where on a little promontory it stood
isolated,
Mark'd how to explore the vacant, vast surrounding,
It launched forth filament, filament, filament, out of
itself,
Ever unreeling them, ever tirelessly speeding them.
And you O my soul where you stand,
Surrounded, detached, in measureless oceans of space,
Ceaselessly musing, venturing, throwing, seeking the
spheres to connect them,
Till the bridge you need be formed, till the ductile
anchor hold,
Till the gossamer thread you fling, catch somewhere,
O my soul.

WALT WHITMAN

HISTORY'S LESSON OF PATIENCE

WE lose the reality of history, we fail to recognize one of the most striking aspects of human affairs, and above all we miss that most invaluable practical lesson, the lesson of patience, unless we remember that the great changes of history took up long periods of time which, when measured by the little life of man, are almost colossal, like the vast changes of geology. We know how long it takes before a species of plant or animal disappears in face of a better adapted

89

Evarra and His Gods

species. Ideas and customs, beliefs and institutions, have always lingered just as long in face of their successors, and the competition is not less keen nor less prolonged, because it is for one or other inevitably destined to be hopeless. History, like geology, demands the use of the imagination, and in proportion as the exercise of the historic imagination is vigorously performed in thinking of the past, will be the breadth of our conception of the changes which the future has in store for us, as well as of the length of time and the magnitude of effort required for their perfect achievement.

JOHN MORLEY
On Compromise

EVARRA AND HIS GODS

Read here,
This is the story of Evarra—man—
Maker of Gods in lands beyond the sea.
    Because the city gave him of her gold,
    Because the caravans brought turquoises,
    Because his life was sheltered by the King,
    So that no man should maim him, none should steal,
    Or break his rest with babble in the streets
    When he was weary after toil, he made
    An image of his God in gold and pearl,
    With turquoise diadem and human eyes,
    A wonder in the sunshine, known afar
    And worshiped by the King ; but, drunk with pride,
    Because the city bowed to him for God,

Evarra and His Gods

He wrote above the shrine : "*Thus Gods are made,*
And whoso makes them otherwise shall die."
And all the city praised him. . . . Then he died.

Read here the story of Evarra—man—
Maker of Gods in lands beyond the sea.
   Because his city had no wealth to give,
   Because the caravans were spoiled afar,
   Because his life was threatened by the King,
   So that all men despised him in the streets,
   He hacked the living rock, with sweat and tears,
   And reared a God against the morning-gold,
   A terror in the sunshine, seen afar,
   And worshiped by the King ; but, drunk with pride,
   Because the city fawned to bring him back,
   He carved upon the plinth : "*Thus Gods are made,*
   And whoso makes them otherwise shall die."
   And all the people praised him. . . Then he died.

Read here the story of Evarra—man—
Maker of Gods in lands beyond the sea.
   Because he lived among a simple folk,
   Because his village was between the hills,
   Because he smeared his cheeks with blood of ewes,
   He cut an idol from a fallen pine,
   Smeared blood upon its cheeks, and wedged a shell
   Above its brows for eyes, and gave it hair
   Of trailing moss, and plaited straw for crown.
   And all the village praised him for his craft,
   And brought him butter, honey, milk, and curds.

Evarra and His Gods

Wherefore, because the shoutings drove him mad,
He scratched upon that log : " *Thus Gods are made,*
And whoso makes them otherwise shall die."
And all the people praised him. . . Then he died.

Read here the story of Evarra—man—
Maker of Gods in lands beyond the sea.
Because his God decreed one clot of blood
Should swerve one hair's-breadth from the pulse's
    path,
And chafe his brain, Evarra mowed alone,
Rag-wrapped, among the cattle in the fields,
Counting his fingers, jesting with the trees,
And mocking at the mist, until his God
Drove him to labor. Out of dung and horns
Dropped in the mire he made a monstrous God,
Abhorrent, shapeless, crowned with plantain tufts,
And when the cattle lowed at twilight time,
He dreamed it was the clamor of lost crowds,
And howled among the beasts : " *Thus Gods are*
    made,
And whoso makes them otherwise shall die."
Thereat the cattle bellowed. . . Then he died.

Yet at the last he came to Paradise,
And found his own four Gods, and that he wrote ;
And marveled, being very near to God,
What oaf on earth had made his toil God's law,
Till God said, mocking : "Mock not. These be thine."
Then cried Evarra : " I have sinned ! "—" Not so.

Thy Joy in Sorrow

If thou hadst written otherwise, thy Gods
Had rested in the mountain and the mine,
And I were poorer by four wondrous Gods,
And thy more wondrous law, Evarra.   Thine,
Servant of shouting crowds and lowing kine."
Thereat with laughing mouth, but tear-wet eyes,
Evarra cast his Gods from Paradise.

This is the story of Evarra—man—
Maker of Gods in lands beyond the sea.

RUDYARD KIPLING

.

THY JOY IN SORROW

GIVE me thy joy in sorrow, gracious Lord,
    And sorrow's self shall like to joy appear !
Although the world should waver in its sphere
I tremble not if Thou thy peace afford ;
But, Thou withdrawn, I am but as a chord
That vibrates to the pulse of hope and fear :
Nor rest I more than harps which to the air
Must answer when we place their tuneful board
Against the blast, which thrill unmeaning woe
Even in their sweetness.   So no earthly wing
E'er sweeps me but to sadden.   Oh, place Thou
My heart beyond the world's sad vibrating—
And where but in Thyself ?   Oh, circle me,
That I may feel no touches save of Thee.

CHAUNCY HARE TOWNSHEND

THUS, at last, out of the old conception of our Bible as a collection of oracles—a mass of entangling utterances, fruitful in wrangling interpretations, which have given to the world long and weary ages of "hatred, malice, and all uncharitableness"; of fetichism, subtlety, and pomp; of tyranny, bloodshed, and solemnly constituted imposture; of everything which the Lord Jesus Christ most abhorred—has been gradually developed through the centuries, by the labors, sacrifices, and even the martyrdom of a long succession of men of God, the conception of it as a sacred literature—a growth only possible under that divine light which the various orbs of science have done so much to bring into the mind and heart and soul of man—a revelation, not of the Fall of Man, but of the Ascent of Man—an exposition, not of temporary dogmas and observances, but of the Eternal Law of Righteousness—the one upward path for individuals and for nations. No longer an oracle, good for the "lower orders" to accept, but to be quietly sneered at by "the enlightened"; no longer a fetich, whose defenders must become persecutors, or reconcilers, or "apologists"; but a most fruitful fact, which religion and science may accept as a source of strength to both.

ANDREW DICKSON WHITE

A History of the Warfare of Science with Theology

BENEATH THIS STARRY ARCH

BENEATH this starry arch
   Naught resteth or is still ;
But all things hold their march,
   As if by one great will :
Moves one, move all: hark to the footfall !
      On, on, for ever !

Yon sheaves were once but seed ;
Will ripens into deed ;
As cave-drops swell the streams,
Day-thoughts feed nightly dreams ;
And sorrow tracketh wrong,
As echo follows song :
      On, on, for ever !

By night, like stars on high,
   The Hours reveal their train ;
They whisper and go by :
   I never watch in vain.
Moves one, move all : hark to the footfall !
      On, on, for ever !

They pass the cradle-head,
And there a promise shed ;
They pass the moist new grave,
And bid rank verdure wave ;
They bear through every clime
The harvests of all time.
      On, on, for ever !

HARRIET MARTINEAU

TACITUS, the historian, thus concludes his life of Agricola, the Roman general, whose son-in-law he was :

" If there be any mansion for the souls of the righteous ; if, as wise men think, great souls be not extinguished with the body, mayest thou rest in peace ; and summon us, thy family, from unavailing regret and effeminate sorrow to the contemplation of those virtues of thine upon which it is not right to bestow either grief or tears. Let us honor thee rather with our admiration than with our short-lived encomiums, and if nature allow it, with our imitation. This is true respect, this is the pious duty of all who are most intimately connected with thee. To thy daughter also, and to thy wife, I should enjoin this, so to revere the memory of the father and of the husband that they may cherish within their hearts all his words and deeds, and retain the form and features of his mind rather than of his person. Not that any restriction be put upon statues which may be made of brass, or marble, but because these, like the human face itself, are frail and perishable, while the form of the mind is eternal. All that we have loved in Agricola, all that we have admired, still remains, and will continue to remain preserved in the minds of men in the succession of ages to remotest posterity."

TO ONE SHORTLY TO DIE

FROM all the rest I single out you, having a message for you,
You are to die—let others tell you what they please, I cannot prevaricate,
I am exact and merciless, but I love you, there is no escape for you.

Softly I lay my right hand upon you, you just feel it,
I do not argue, I bend my head close, and half envelop it,
I sit quietly by, I remain faithful,
I am more than nurse, more than parent or neighbor,
I absolve you from all except yourself, spiritual bodily,
That is eternal, you yourself will surely escape,
The corpse you will leave will be but excrementitious.

The sun bursts through in unlooked-for-directions,
Strong thoughts fill you, and confidence, you smile,
You forget you are sick, as I forget you are sick,
You do not see the medicines, you do not mind the weeping friends, I am with you,
I exclude others from you, there is nothing to be commiserated,
I do not commiserate, I congratulate you.

WALT WHITMAN

IMMORTALITY

SO when the old delight is born anew,
　　And God re-animates the early bliss,
Seems it not all as one first trembling kiss
Ere soul knew soul with whom she has to do ?
　O nights how desolate, O days how few,
　O death in life, if life be this, be this !
　O weigh'd alone as one shall win or miss
The faint eternity which shines therethro' !
　Lo, all that age is as a speck of sand
Lost on the long beach where the tides are free,
　And no man metes it in his hollow hand
Nor cares to ponder it, how small it be ;
　At ebb it lies forgotten on the land,
And at full tide forgotten in the sea.

FREDERIC WILLIAM HENRY MYERS

EVIL IS NECESSARY

EVIL is necessary. If it did not exist, the good
would not exist. Evil is the unique reason for
the good's being. What would courage be far from
peril, and what pity without pain ? What would become of devotion and sacrifice if happiness were universal ? It is because of evil and suffering that the
earth may be inhabited and that life is worth living.
For every vice that you destroy there is a correspond-
ing virtue that perishes with it.

ANATOLE FRANCE

THE TOUCH OF LIFE

I SAW a circle in a garden sit
    Of dainty dames and solemn cavaliers,
Whereof some shuddered at the burrowing nit,
    And at the carrion worm some burst in tears :
And all, as envying the abhorred estate
    Of empty shades and disembodied elves,
Under the laughing stars, early and late,
    Sat shamefast at their birth and at themselves.
The keeper of the house of life is fear ;
In the rent lion is the honey found
By him that rent it ; out of stony ground
    The toiler, in the morning of the year,
Beholds the harvest of his grief abound
    And the green corn put forth the tender ear.

ROBERT LOUIS STEVENSON

RATIONALISM

THE word "Rationalism" has the misfortune, shared by most words in this gray world, of being somewhat equivocal. This evil may be overcome by careful preliminary definition ; but Mr. Lecky does not supply this, and the original specific application of the word to a particular phase of Biblical interpretation seems to have clung about his use of it with a misleading effect. Through some parts of his book ("The Influence of Rationalism") he appears to regard the grand characteristic of modern thought and civilization, compared with ancient, as a radiation in the first instance from a change in religious conceptions. The supremely important fact, that the reduction of all phenomena within the sphere of established law, which carries as a consequence the rejection of the miraculous, has its determining current in the development of physical science, seems to have engaged comparatively little of his attention ; at least, he gives it no prominence. The great conception of universal regular sequence, without partiality and without caprice—the conception which is the most potent force at work in the modification of our faith, and of the practical form given to our sentiments—could only grow out of that patient watching of external fact, and that silencing of preconceived notions, which are urged upon the mind by the problems of physical science.

GEORGE ELIOT
Essay on Lecky's " Influence of Rationalism "

A CHRYSALIS

WHEN gathering shells cast upward by the
    waves
  Of Progress, they who note its ebb and flow,
  Its flux and reflux, surely come to know
That the sea-level rises ; that dark caves
Of ignorance are flooded, and foul graves
  Of sin are cleansed ; albeit the work is slow ;
  Till, seeing great from less forever grow,
Law comes to mean for them the Love that saves !
And leaning down the ages, my dull ear,

God-Seeking

Catching their slow-ascending harmonies,
I am uplift by them, and borne more near,
  I feel within my flesh—laid pupa-wise—
A soul of worship, tho' of vision dim,
Which links me with wing-folded cherubim.

EMILY PFEIFFER

GOD-SEEKING

G OD-SEEKING thou hast journeyed far and nigh,
    On dawn-lit mountain-tops thy soul did yearn
To hear His trailing garments wander by ;
    And where 'mid thunderous glooms great sunsets
            burn,
Vainly thou sought'st His shadow on sea and sky ;
    Or gazing up, at noontide, could'st discern
Only a neutral heaven's indifferent eye
    And countenance austerely taciturn.
Yet whom thou soughtest I have found at last,
    Neither where tempest dims the world below,
Nor where the westering daylight reels aghast
    In conflagrations of red overthrow :
But where this virgin brooklet silvers past,
    And yellowing either bank the king-cups blow.

WILLIAM WATSON

SLEEP

WHEN to soft sleep we give ourselves away,
    And in a dream as in a fairy bark
Drift on and on through the enchanted dark
To purple daybreak—little thought we pay
To that sweet bitter world we know by day.
We are clean quit of it, as is a lark
So high in heaven no human eye can mark
The thin swift pinion cleaving through the gray.
Till we awake ill fate can do no ill,
The resting heart shall not take up again
The heavy load that yet must make it bleed ;
For this brief space the loud world's voice is still,
No faintest echo of it brings us pain.
How will it be when we shall sleep indeed ?

THOMAS BAILEY ALDRICH

HOW LITTLE OF OURSELVES WE KNOW

HOW little of ourselves we know
    Before a grief the heart has felt !
The lessons that we learn of woe
    May brace the mind as well as melt.

The energies too stern for mirth,
    The reach of thought, the strength of will,
'Mid cloud and tempest have their birth,
    Through blight and blast, their course fulfill.

And yet 'tis when it mourns and fears,
  The loaded spirit feels forgiven;
And through the mist of falling tears
  We catch the clearest glimpse of heaven.

LORD MORPETH

PAST AND FUTURE

FAIR garden, where the man and woman dwelt,
    And loved, and worked, and where, in work's
      reprieve,
  The sabbath of each day, the restful eve,
They sat in silence, with locked hands, and felt
The voice which compassed them, a-near, a-far,
  Which murmured in the fountains and the breeze,
  Which breathed in spices from the laden trees,
And sent a silvery shout from each lone star.
Sweet dream of Paradise! and it a dream,
  One that has helped us when our faith was weak;
We wake, and still it holds us, but would seem
  Before us, not behind,—the good we seek,—
The good from lowest root which waxes ever,
The golden age of science and endeavor.

EMILY PFEIFFER

WE may not be doomed
      To cope with seraphs, but at least the rest
Shall cope with us.   Make no more giants, God,
But elevate the race at once ! We ask
To put forth just our strength, our human strength,
All starting fairly, all equipped alike,
Gifted alike, all eagle-eyed, true-hearted—
See if we cannot beat Thine angels yet !
Such is my task.   I go to gather this
The sacred knowledge, here and there dispersed
About the world, long lost or never found.
And why should I be sad or lorn of hope ?
Why ever make man's good distinct from God's,
Or, finding they are one, why dare mistrust ?
Who shall succeed if not one pledged like me ?
Mine is no mad attempt to build a world
Apart from His, like those who set themselves
To find the nature of the spirit they bore,
And, taught betimes that all their gorgeous dreams
Were only born to vanish in this life,
Refused to fit them to its narrow sphere,
But chose to figure forth another world
And other frames meet for their vast desires—
And all a dream ?

ROBERT BROWNING
Paracelsus

IF IT SHOULD BE WE ARE WATCHED UNAWARE

IF it should be we are watched unaware
    By those who are gone from us ; if our sighs
    Ring in their ears ; if tears that scald our eyes
They see and long to stanch ; if our despair

Fills them with anguish,—we must learn to bear
    In strength of silence.   Howso doubt denies
    It cannot give assurance which defies
All peradventure ; and if anywhere

Our loved grieve with our ˉgrieving, cruel we
    To cherish selfishness of woe.   The chance
Should keep us steadfast.   Tortured utterly,

This hope alone in all the world's expanse
    We clutch forlornly ; how deep love can be,
Grief's silence proving more than utterance.

ARLO BATES
Sonnets in Shadow

MIRACLES GOING OUT

ALTHOUGH an educated Protestant may man-
age to retain for his own lifetime the belief in
miracles in which he was brought up, yet his children will
lose it ; so to an educated Catholic we may say, putting
the change only a little further off, that (unless some
unforseen deluge should overwhelm European civiliza-

tion, leaving everything to be begun anew) his grand-children will lose it. They will lose it insensibly, as the eighteenth century saw the gradual extinction, among the educated classes, of that belief in witchcraft which in the century previous, a man like Sir Matthew Hale could affirm to have the authority of Scripture and of the wisdom of all nations,—spoke of, in short, just as many religious people speak of miracles now. Witchcraft is but one department of the miraculous; and it was comparatively easy, no doubt, to abandon one department, when men had all the rest of the re-gion to fall back upon. Nevertheless, the forces of experience, which have prevailed against witchcraft will inevitably prevail also against miracles at large, and that by the mere progress of time.

MATTHEW ARNOLD
God and the Bible

SAY NOT, THE STRUGGLE NAUGHT AVAILETH

SAY not, the struggle naught availeth,
    The labor and the wounds are vain,
The enemy faints not, nor faileth,
    And as things have been they remain.

If hopes were dupes, fears may be liars ;
    It may be, in yon smoke concealed,
Your comrades chase e'en now the fliers,
    And, but for you, possess the field.

Self-Dependence

For while the tired waves, vainly breaking,
   Seem here no painful inch to gain,
Far back, through creeks and inlets making,
   Comes silent, flooding in, the main.

And not by eastern windows only,
   When daylight comes, comes in the light,
In front, the sun climbs slow, how slowly,
   But westward, look, the land is bright.
                ARTHUR HUGH CLOUGH

SELF-DEPENDENCE

WEARY of myself, and sick of asking
   What I am, and what I ought to be,
At the vessel's prow I stand, which bears me
Forward, forward, o'er the starlit sea.

And a look of passionate desire
O'er the sea and to the stars I send :
"Ye who from my childhood up have calm'd me,
Calm me, ah, compose me to the end.

" Ah, once more," I cried, " ye Stars, ye Waters,
On my heart your mighty charm renew :
Still, still let me, as I gaze upon you,
Feel my soul becoming vast like you."

From the intense, clear, star-sown vault of heaven,
Over the lit sea's unquiet way,
In the rustling night-air came the answer—
" Wouldst thou *be* as they are ? *Live as* they.

Autumn

"Unaffrighted by the silence round them,
Undistracted by the sights they see,
These demand not that the things without them
Yield them love, amusement, sympathy.

"And with joy the stars perform their shining,
And the sea its long moon-silvered roll.
For alone they live, nor pine with noting
All the fever of some differing soul.

"Bounded by themselves and unobservant
In what state God's other works may be,
In their own tasks all their own powers pouring,
These attain the mighty life you see."

O air-born voice ! long since, severely clear
A cry like thine in my own heart I hear.
"Resolve to be thyself : and know, that he
Who finds himself, loses his misery."

MATTHEW ARNOLD

AUTUMN

NOW Autumn's fire burns slowly along the woods,
    And day by day the dead leaves fall and melt,
And night by night the monitory blast
Wails in the key-hole, telling how it pass'd
O'er empty fields, or upland solitudes,
Or grim wide wave ; and now the power is felt
Of melancholy, tenderer in its moods
Than any joy indulgent summer dealt.

God is not Dumb

Dear friends, together in the glimmering eve,
Pensive and glad, with tones that recognize
The soft invisible dew in each one's eyes,
It may be, somewhat thus we shall have leave
To walk with memory, when distant lies
Poor earth, where we were wont to live and grieve.

WILLIAM ALLINGHAM

GOD IS NOT DUMB

GOD is not dumb, that he should speak no more ;
⸱If thou hast wanderings in the wilderness
And find'st not Sinai, 'tis thy soul is poor ;
  There towers the mountain of the Voice no less,
Which whoso seeks shall find ; but he who bends
Intent on manna still, and mortal ends,
  Sees it not, neither hears its thundered lore.

Slowly the Bible of the race is writ,
  And not on paper leaves, nor leaves of stone ;
Each age, each kindred, adds a verse to it,
  Texts of despair or hope, of joy or moan.
While swings the sea, while mists the mountains shroud,
While thunder's surges burst on cliffs of cloud,
  Still at the prophets' feet the nations sit.

JAMES RUSSELL LOWELL
Bibliolatres

TEARS

NOT in the time of pleasure
    Hope doth set her bow ;
But in the sky of sorrow,
Over the vale of woe.

Through gloom and shadow look we
On beyond the years ;
The soul would have no rainbow
Had the eyes no tears.

JOHN VANCE CHENEY

THE WORLD'S ADVANCE

JUDGE mildly the tasked world ; and disincline
    To brand it, for it bears a heavy pack.
You have perchance observed the inebriate's track
At night when he has quitted the inn-sign :
He plays diversions on the homeward line,
    Still *that* way bent albeit his legs are slack :
    A hedge may take him but he turns not back.
Nor turns this burdened world, of curving spine :
    "Spiral," the memorable lady terms,
Our mind's ascent : our world's advance presents
    That figure on a flat ;—the way of worms.
Cherish the promise of its good intents,
    And warn it not one instinct to efface
    Till reason ripens for the vacant place.

GEORGE MEREDITH

THE LAND BEYOND THE SEA

THE land beyond the sea!
   When will life's tasks be o'er?
When shall we reach that soft blue shore,
O'er the dark strait whose billows foam and roar?
   When shall we come to thee,
   Calm Land beyond the Sea?

The Land beyond the Sea!
How close it often seems,
When flushed with evening's peaceful gleams;
And the wistful heart looks o'er the strait, and dreams!
   It longs to fly to thee,
   Calm Land beyond the Sea!

The Land beyond the Sea!
How dark our present home!
By the dull beach and sullen foam
How wearily, how drearily we roam,
   With arms outstretched to thee,
   Calm Land beyond the Sea!

The Land beyond the Sea!
Why fadest thou in light?
Why art thou better seen toward night?
Dear Land! look always plain, look always bright,
   That we may gaze on thee,
   Calm Land beyond the Sea!

                         FREDERICK WILLIAM FABER

INFIDELITY

WHO is the infidel, but he who fears
  To face the utmost truth, whate'er it be ?
Dreads God the light ? and is his majesty
A shadow that in sunshine disappears ?
Or leads he in the swift-ascending years
 Into a light where men may plainer see ?
 He trusts him best to whom the mystery
Hides nothing dangerous ; who ever hears,
With faith unshaken, his new uttered voice,
 And knows it cannot contradict the truth
  It in the old time spoke. Whate'er it saith,
He fears not then, but bids his heart rejoice,
 In old age trustful as he was in youth.
  This only, though called infidel, is faith.

MINOT JUDSON SAVAGE

Duty Here and Now

Conduct is three-fourths of life.
MATTHEW ARNOLD

So live, that when thy summons comes to join
The innumerable caravan which moves
To that mysterious realm where each shall take
His chamber in the silent halls of death,
Thou go not like the quarry-slave at night,
Scourged to his dungeon ; but sustained and soothed
By an unfaltering trust, approach thy grave
Like one who wraps the drapery of his couch
About him, and lies down to pleasant dreams.
WILLIAM CULLEN BRYANT
Thanatopsis

BE STRONG AND OF GOOD COURAGE

WHAT do you think of yourself? What do you think of the world? . . . These are questions with which all must deal as it seems good to them. They are riddles of the Sphinx, and in some way or other we must deal with them. . . . In all important transactions of life we have to take a leap in the dark. . . . If we decide to leave the riddles unanswered, that is a choice; if we waver in our answer, that, too, is a choice; but whatever choice we make, we make it at our peril. If a man chooses to turn his back altogether on God and the future, no one can prevent him; no one can show beyond reasonable doubt that he is mistaken. If a man thinks otherwise and acts as he thinks, I do not see that any one can prove that *he* is mistaken. Each must act as he thinks best; and if he is wrong, so much the worse for him. We stand on a mountain pass in the midst of whirling snow and blinding mist, through which we get glimpses now and then of paths which may be deceptive. If we stand still we shall be frozen to death. If we take the wrong road we shall be dashed to pieces. We do not certainly know whether there is any right one. What must we do? "Be strong and of good courage." Act for the best, hope for the best, and take what comes. If death ends all, we cannot meet death better.

JAMES FITZ JAMES STEPHEN
Liberty, Equality, Fraternity

115

NOTHING WALKS WITH AIMLESS FEET

IF Sleep and Death be truly one,
   And every spirit's folded bloom
   Thro' all its intervital gloom
In some long trance should slumber on ;

Unconscious of the sliding hour,
   Bare of the body, might it last,
   And silent traces of the past
Be all the color of the flower :

So then were nothing lost to man ;
   But that still garden of the souls
   In many a figured leaf enrolls
The total world since life began :

And love would last as pure and whole
   As when he loved me here in Time,
   And at the spiritual prime
Rewaken with the dawning soul.

O yet we trust that somehow good
   Will be the final goal of ill,
   To pangs of nature, sins of will,
Defects of doubt, and taints of blood ;

That nothing walks with aimless feet ;
   That not one life shall be destroy'd,
   Or cast as rubbish to the void,
When God hath made the pile complete ;

Scientific Grounds for Right Conduct

That not a worm is cloven in vain ;
  That not a moth with vain desire
  Is shrivel'd in a fruitless fire,
Or but subserves another's gain.

Behold, we know not anything ;
  I can but trust that good shall fall
  At last—far off—at last, to all,
And every winter change to spring.

So runs my dream : but what am I ?
  An infant crying in the night :
  An infant crying for the light :
And with no language but a cry.
                ALFRED, LORD TENNYSON
                        In Memoriam

SCIENTIFIC GROUNDS FOR RIGHT CONDUCT

THE establishment of rules of right conduct on a scientific basis is a pressing need. Now that moral injunctions are losing the authority given by their supposed sacred origin, the secularization of morals is becoming imperative. Few things can happen more disastrous than the decay and death of a regulative system no longer fit, before another and fitter regulative system has grown up to replace it. Most of those who reject the current creed, appear to assume that the controlling agency furnished by it may safely be thrown aside, and the vacancy left unfilled by any other controlling agency. Meanwhile, those who defend the current creed allege that, in the absence of the guidance it yields, no guidance can exist: divine commandments they think the only possible guides. Thus between these extreme opponents there is a certain community. The one holds that the gap left by disappearance of the code of supernatural ethics need not be filled by a code of natural ethics ; and the other holds that it cannot be so filled. Both contemplate a vacuum, which the one wishes and the other fears. As the change which promises or threatens to bring about this state, desired or dreaded, is rapidly progressing, those who believe that the vacuum can be filled, and that it must be filled, are called upon to do something in pursuance of their belief.

HERBERT SPENCER

Preface to "The Data of Ethics "

THE PRAYER-SEEKER

ALONG the aisle where prayer was made.
　　A woman, all in black arrayed,
Close-veiled, between the kneeling host,
With gliding motion of a ghost,
Passed to the desk, and laid thereon
A scroll which bore these words alone,
　　　　　Pray for me !

The Prayer-seeker

Back from the place of worshiping
She glided like a guilty thing :
The rustle of her draperies stirred
By hurrying feet, alone was heard ;
While full of awe, the preacher read,
As out into the dark she sped :
                    " Pray for me ! "

Back to the night from whence she came,
To unimagined grief or shame !
Across the threshold of that door
None knew the burden that she bore ;
Alone she left the written scroll,
The legend of a troubled soul,—
                    Pray for me !

Glide on, poor ghost of woe or sin !
Thou leav'st a common need within ;
Each bears, like thee, some nameless weight,
Some misery inarticulate,
Some secret sin, some shrouded dread,
Some household sorrow all unsaid.
                    Pray for us !

Pass on ! The type of all thou art,
Sad witness to the human heart !
With face in veil and seal on lip,
In mute and strange companionship,
Like thee we wander to and fro,
Humbly imploring as we go :
                    Pray for us !

The Prayer-seeker

Ah, who shall pray, since he who pleads
Our want perchance hath greater needs?
Yet they who make their loss the gain
Of others shall not ask in vain,
And heaven bends low to hear the prayer
Of love from lips of self-despair:
>   *Pray for us!*

In vain remorse and fear and hate
Beat with bruised hands against a fate
Whose walls of iron only move
And open to the touch of love.
He only feels his burdens fall
Who, taught by suffering, pities all.
>   *Pray for us!*

He prayeth best who leaves unguessed
The mystery of another's breast.
Why cheeks grow pale, why eyes o'erflow,
Or heads are white, thou need'st not know.
Enough to note by many a sign
That every heart hath needs like thine.
>   *Pray for us!*
>   JOHN GREENLEAF WHITTIER

IN making false notions the proofs or close associates of true ones, you are exposing the latter to the ruin which awaits the former. If you have in the minds of children or servants associated honesty, industry, truthfulness, with the fear of hell-fire, then supposing this fear to become extinct in their minds,— which, being unfounded in truth, it is in constant risk of doing—the virtues associated with it are likely to be weakened in proportion as that association was strong.

For all good habits in thought or conduct there are good and real reasons in the nature of things. To leave such habits attached to false opinions is to lessen the weight of these natural or spontaneous reasons, and so to do more harm in the long run, than effacement of them seems for a time to do good. Most excellences in human character have a spontaneous root in our nature. Moreover, if they had not, and where they have not, there is always a valid and real defense for them. The unreal defense must be weaker than the real one, and the substitution of a weak for a strong defense, where both are to be had, is not useful but the very opposite.
JOHN MORLEY
On Compromise

DAYS

DAUGHTERS of Time, the hypocritic Days,
    Muffled and dumb like barefoot dervishes,
And marching single in an endless file,
Bring diadems and fagots in their hands.
To each they offer gifts after his will,
Bread, kingdoms, stars, and sky that holds them all.
I, in my pleached garden, watched the pomp,
Forgot my morning wishes, hastily
Took a few herbs and apples, and the Day
Turned and departed silent. I, too late,
Under her solemn fillet saw the scorn.
RALPH WALDO EMERSON

RELIGION AND CONDUCT

THOUGH the decay of religion may leave the institutes of morality intact, it drains off their inward power. The devout faith of men expresses and measures the intensity of their moral nature, and it cannot be lost without a remission of enthusiasm, and under this low pressure, the successful re-entrance of importunate desires and clamorous passions which had been driven back. To believe in an ever-living and perfect Mind, supreme over the universe, is to invest moral distinctions with immensity and eternity, and lift them from the provincial stage of human society to the imperishable theater of all being. When planted thus

The Law of Love

in the very substance of things, they justify and support the ideal estimates of the conscience; they deepen every guilty shame; they guarantee every righteous hope; and they keep the will with a divine casting-vote in every balance of temptation. The sanctity thus given to the claims of duty, and the interest that gathers around the play of character, appear to me more important elements in the power of religion than its direct sanctions of hope and fear. Yet to these also it is hardly possible to deny great weight, not only as extending the range of personal interests, but as the answer of reality to the retributory verdicts of the moral sense. Cancel these beliefs, and morality will be left reasonable still, but paralyzed; possible to temperaments comparatively passionless, but with no grasp on vehement and poetic natures; and gravitating to the simply prudential wherever it maintains its ground.

JAMES MARTINEAU

The Influence upon Morality of a Decline in Religious Belief

THE LAW OF LOVE

MAKE channels for the streams of love,
    Where they may broadly run;
And love has overflowing streams,
    To fill them every one.

Progress Not Automatic

But if at any time we cease
 Such channels to provide,
The very founts of love for us
 Will soon be parched and dried.

For we must share, if we would keep
 That blessing from above ;
Ceasing to give, we cease to have—
 Such is the law of love.

RICHARD CHENEVIX TRENCH

PROGRESS NOT AUTOMATIC

IT would be odd if the theory which makes progress depend on modification, forbade us to attempt to modify. When it is said that the various successive changes in thought and institution present and consummate themselves spontaneously, no one means by spontaneity that they come to pass independently of human effort and volition. On the contrary, this energy of the members of the society is one of the spontaneous elements. It is quite as indispensable as any other of them, if, indeed, it be not more so. Progress depends upon tendencies and forces in a community. But of these tendencies and forces, the organs and representatives must plainly be found among the men and women of the community, and cannot possibly be found anywhere else. Progress is not automatic, in the sense that if we were all cast into a deep slumber for the space of a generation, we should awake to find ourselves in a greatly improved social state. The world only grows better, even in the moderate degree in which it does grow better, because people wish that it should, and take the right steps to make it better. Evolution is not a force, but a process; not a cause, but a law. It explains the source, and marks the immovable limitations of social energy. But social energy itself can never be superseded either by evolution or by anything else.

JOHN MORLEY
On Compromise

STARLIGHT

THEY think me daft, who nightly meet
My face turned starward, while my feet
Stumble along the unseen street ;

But should man's thoughts have only room
For earth, his cradle and his tomb,
Not for his Temple's grander gloom ?

And must the prisoner all his days
Learn but his dungeon's narrow ways
And never through its grating gaze ?

Then let me linger in your sight,
My only amaranths ! blossoming bright
As over Eden's cloudless night,

Starlight

The same vast belt, and square, and crown,
That on the Deluge glittered down,
And lit the roofs of Bethlehem town !

Ye make me one with all my race,
A victor over time and space,
Till all the path of men I pace.

Far-speeding backward in my brain
We build the Pyramids again,
And Babel rises from the plain ;

And climbing upward on your beams
I peer within the Patriarch's dreams,
Till the deep sky with angels teems.

My comforters !—Yea, why not mine ?
The power that kindled you doth shine,
In man, a mastery divine ;

That love which throbs in every star,
And quickens all the worlds afar,
Beats warmer where his children are.

The shadow of the wings of Death
Broods over us ; we feel his breath :
" Resurgam " still the spirit saith.

These tired feet, this weary brain,
Blotted with many a mortal stain,
May crumble earthward—not in vain.

The Frost Palace

With swifter feet that shall not tire,
Eyes that shall fail not at your fire,
Nearer your splendors I aspire.

EDWARD ROWLAND SILL

THE FROST PALACE

SINCE the theological buttresses of morals are giving way, the question is anxiously pressed, What is to take their place? The answer must be that morals derive their real authority from the facts of nature and of life. Truthfulness, sobriety, industry, and the rest, are rewarded here and now in most cases. In the few cases where they are not rewarded, why blink the fact? It is a fact which may purge the good man's record of the taunt that he does right for wages,—although at the same time it tempts the evil man to do wrong from which he may escape scathless. Let it be remembered, too, that most of the right in the world is of good men's making, and that there will be more when they make more—as they easily can. A theology which has laid undue stress on generosity has laid too little upon justice. Let us put our sympathy in the right place, and instead of pitying the thief and drunkard and murderer so much, begin to pity their victims, and meanwhile do what we can to make thieves, drunkards, and murderers impossible. Christianity still bears the stamp of its primitive days, when the Christian cowered before the pagan, and virtue trampled in the dust postponed its visions of peace

The Frost Palace

and triumph to a sphere beyond the stars. To this day we have a thousand Crucifixions to one Ascension.

But the teachers of right living can to-day be strong, not cowering and afraid. Such discordances as still exist between earning and having shall disappear just so soon as the people realize their power to remake the institutions which retain so much of the injustice of the past. Institutions are for men, not men for institutions. In abating the evils of Property, and much else, an enlightened ballot has great tasks before it.

Religious men need feel no fear. Their neighbors do not change one set of convictions for another unless they believe the new to be truer than the old. Illusion dies no faster than Fact is recognized as more worthy of place.

A few years ago it was the pleasure of the young people of a Canadian city to build their first palace of ice in one of their public squares. Its proportions were magnificent, its effect one of spectral beauty. When the structure was doomed to melt in the rays of the sunbeams of spring, there was not a little apprehension. "What will befall the neighborhood?" was asked, "when these massy walls and columns are dissolved?" What was the fact? Day by day a gentle thaw did its work so quietly that the ice blocks might have been chiseled stone for all the hurt they did. The thirsty ground drank in every drop of liquid as fast as it fell. The frost palace vanished even more gracefully than it first arose at the architect's bidding.

HENRY ALLEN BLISS

IF I SHOULD DIE TO-NIGHT

IF I should die to-night,
　　My friends would look upon my quiet face
Before they laid it in its resting-place,
And deem that death had left it almost fair ;
And, laying snow-white flowers against my hair,
Would smooth it down with tearful tenderness,
And fold my hands with lingering caress,—
Poor hands, so empty and so cold to-night !

If I should die to-night,
My friends would call to mind, with loving thought,
Some kindly deed the icy hands had wrought ;
Some gentle word the frozen lips had said ;
Errands on which the willing feet had sped ;
The memory of my selfishness and pride,
My hasty words, would all be put aside,
And so I should be loved and mourned to-night.

If I should die to-night,
Even hearts estranged would turn once more to me,
Recalling other days remorsefully ;
The eyes that chill me with averted glance
Would look upon me as of yore, perchance,
And soften, in the old familiar way ;
For who could war with dumb, unconscious clay !
So I might rest, forgiven of all, to-night.

The Golden Rule

Oh, friends, I pray to-night,
Keep not your kisses for my dead, cold brow—
The way is lonely, let me feel them now.
Think gently of me ; I am travel-worn ;
My faltering feet are pierced with many a thorn.
Forgive, oh, hearts estranged, forgive, I plead !
When dreamless rest is mine I shall not need
The tenderness for which I long to-night.

ARABELLA E. SMITH

THE GOLDEN RULE

MORALISTS of all ages and of all faiths, attending only to the relations of men towards one another in an ideal society, have agreed upon the "golden rule," "Do as you would be done by." In other words, let sympathy be your guide, put yourself in the place of the man toward whom your action is directed ; and do to him what you would like to have done to yourself under the circumstances. However much one may admire the generosity of such a rule of conduct ; however confident one may be that average men may be thoroughly depended upon not to carry it out in its full logical consequences ; it is nevertheless desirable to recognize the fact that these consequences are incompatible with the existence of a civil state, under any circumstances of this world which have obtained, or, so far as one can see, are likely to come to pass.

For I imagine there can be no doubt that the great desire of every wrongdoer is to escape from the painful

The Golden Rule

consequences of his actions. If I put myself in the place of the man who has robbed me, I find that I am possessed by an exceeding desire not to be fined or imprisoned ; if in that of the man who has smitten me on one cheek, I contemplate with satisfaction the absence of any worse result than the turning of the other cheek for like treatment. Strictly observed, the "golden rule" involves the negation of law by the refusal to put it in motion against law-breakers ; and, as regards the external relations of a polity, it is the refusal to continue the struggle for existence. It can be obeyed, even partially, only under the protection of a society which repudiates it. Without such shelter, the followers of the "golden rule" may indulge in hopes of heaven, but they must reckon with the certainty that other people will be masters of the earth.

What would become of the garden if the gardener treated all the weeds and slugs and birds and trespassers as he would like to be treated, if he were in their place ?

THOMAS HENRY HUXLEY
Evolution and Ethics

EVOLUTION

HUNGER that strivest in the restless arms
  Of the sea-flower, that drivest rooted things
  To break their moorings, that unfoldest wings
In creatures to be rapt above thy harms ;
Hunger, of whom the hungry-seeming waves
  Were the first ministers, till, free to range,
  Thou mad'st the Universe thy park and grange,
What is it thine insatiate heart still craves ?
Sacred disquietude, divine unrest !
  Maker of all that breathes the breath of life,
No unthrift greed spurs thine unflagging zest,
  No lust self-slaying hounds thee to the strife ;
Thou art the Unknown God on whom we wait ;
Thy path the course of our unfolded fate.

EMILY PFEIFFER

THE RIGHT MUST WIN

OH, it is hard to work for God,
  To rise and take His part
Upon this battle-field of earth,
  And not sometimes lose heart !

He hides Himself so wondrously,
  As though there were no God ;
He is least seen when all the powers
  Of ill are most abroad.

The Right Must Win

Or he deserts us at the hour
  The fight is all but lost ;
And seems to leave us to ourselves
  Just when we need Him most.

Ill masters good ; good seems to change
  To ill with greatest ease ;
And, worst of all, the good with good
  Is at cross-purposes.

Ah ! God is other than we think ;
  His ways are far above,
Far beyond reason's height, and reach'd
  Only by child-like love.

Workman of God ! Oh, lose not heart,
  But learn what God is like ;
And in the darkest battle-field
  Thou shalt know where to strike.

Thrice bless'd is he to whom is given
  The instinct that can tell
That God is on the field when He
  Is most invisible.

Bless'd, too, is he who can divine
  Where real right doth lie,
And dares to take the side that seems
  Wrong to man's blindfold eye.

An Angel in the House

For right is right, since God is God ;
   And right the day must win ;
To doubt would be disloyalty,
   To falter would be sin.
FREDERICK WILLIAM FABER

AN ANGEL IN THE HOUSE

HOW sweet it were if, without fright,
   Or dying of the beauteous sight,
An angel came to us, and we could bear
To see him issue from the silent air
At evening in our room, and bend on ours
His divine eyes, and bring us from his bowers
   News of dear children who have never
   Been dead indeed—as we shall know for ever.
Alas ! we think not that we daily see
About our hearths—angels that *are* to be,
   Or may be if they will, and we prepare
   Their souls and ours to meet in happy air ;
A child, a friend, a wife, whose soft heart sings
In unison with ours, breeding its future wings.
LEIGH HUNT

"OH, MAY I JOIN THE CHOIR INVISIBLE"

OH, may I join the choir invisible
  Of those immortal dead who live again
In minds made better by their presence : live
In pulses stirr'd to generosity,
In deeds of daring, rectitude, in scorn
For miserable aims that end with self,
In thoughts sublime that pierce the night like stars,
And with their mild persistence urge man's search
To vaster issues.
              So to live in heaven :
To make undying music in the world,
Breathing as beauteous order that controls
With growing sway the growing life of man.
So we inherit that sweet purity
For which we struggled, fail'd, and agoniz'd
With widening retrospect that bred despair.
Rebellious flesh that would not be subdued,
A vicious parent shaming still its child,
Poor anxious penitence, is quick dissolv'd ;
Its discords, quenched by meeting harmonies,
Die in the large and charitable air.
And all our rarer, better, truer self,
That sobb'd religiously in yearning song,
That watch'd to ease the burthen of the world,
Laboriously tracing what must be,
And what may yet be better,—saw within
A worthier image for the sanctuary,
And shaped it forth before the multitude,

Why False Dogmas Survive

Divinely human, raising worship so
To higher reverence more mix'd with love,—
That better self shall live till human Time
Shall fold its eyelids, and the human sky
Be gather'd like a scroll within the tomb
Unread forever.
                    This is life to come,
Which martyr'd men have made more glorious
For us who strive to follow.   May I reach
That purest heaven, be to other souls
The cup of strength in some great agony,
Enkindle generous ardor, feed pure love,
Beget the smiles that have no cruelty,
Be the sweet presence of a good diffus'd,
And in diffusion ever more intense !
So shall I join the choir invisible
Whose music is the gladness of the world.

GEORGE ELIOT

WHY FALSE DOGMAS SURVIVE

NO doubt history abounds with cases in which a false opinion on moral or religious subjects, or an erroneous motive in conduct, has seemed to be a stepping-stone to truth.   But this is in no sense a demonstration of the utility of error.   For in all such cases the erroneous opinion or motive was far from being wholly erroneous, or wholly without elements of truth and reality.   If it helped to quicken the speed or mend the direction of progress, that must have been by virtue of some such elements within it. All that was error in it was pure waste, or worse than waste. It is true that the religious sentiment has clothed itself in a great number of unworthy, inadequate, depressing, and otherwise misleading shapes, dogmatic and liturgic. Yet, on the whole, the religious sentiment has conferred enormous benefits on civilization. This is no proof of the utility of the mistaken direction which these dogmatic or liturgic shapes imposed upon it. On the contrary, the effect of the false dogmas and enervating liturgies is so much that has to be deducted from the advantages conferred by a sentiment in itself valuable and of priceless capability.

JOHN MORLEY
On Compromise

ON LIFE'S ROUGH SEA

GIVE me a spirit that on this life's rough sea
    Loves to have his sails filled with a lusty wind,
Even till his sail-yards tremble, his masts crack,
And his rapt ship runs on her side so low
That she drinks water, and her keel plows air.
There is no danger to a man that knows
What life and death is,—there's not any law
Exceeds his knowledge ; neither is it lawful
That he should stoop to any other law.

GEORGE CHAPMAN

MORALITY AND THEISM

THE authors of systems of moral philosophy have sought to discover some intellectual principle from which all moral rules could be logically deduced, the apprehension of which would constrain all men to be moral. But the question remains, why men who do not like to be moral, as many men do not, are to sacrifice their propensities to a logical deduction from an intellectual principle. Suppose virtue to correspond, as Clarke says, to the fitness of things, why is Borgia to prefer the fitness of things to the enjoyment of his orgies and to the criminal courses by which the means of that enjoyment are to be obtained ? What is needed to influence the actions of men is not an abstract principle or a definition, but a motive. It is by renewing and reinforcing the motive power, not by defining morality, that the great moral reforms and movements have been made. Desire of health, of domestic happiness, of the esteem and good-will of our fellows, of the security for our lives and property which we must purchase by reciprocal respect for the lives and property of others, and by obedience to the laws, are motive powers. The necessity of obeying the will of God, with eternal reward or punishment annexed, on which Paley founds the inducement to virtue, provided the truth of theism can be proved, is a motive power of the most overwhelming kind. Intellectual perception of the fitness of things is not.

138

Morality and Theism

If no divine command for the practice of virtue can be shown, if no assurance of the virtuous man's reward, such as Paley assumes, can be given, moral philosophy must, it would appear, be content simply to take the observation of human nature as its basis and to build its system on the natural desires of man, offering them such satisfaction as is consistent with the welfare of the community and the race. We naturally desire health, and to be healthy means to be temperate and continent ; we desire, for ourselves and our families, the means of living, and to obtain them we must be industrious, frugal, and of good repute ; we desire domestic happiness, and to obtain it we must practice the domestic virtues ; we desire the good-will of our fellow-men with the advantages which it brings, and to obtain it we must practice the virtues of good members of society and good citizens. There is no such thing as altruism in the literal sense of that term. Self is present in all we do, though the self is that of a being who desires love and fellowship as well as food and raiment ; with which qualification the philosophy which has resolved morality into self-interest, though much decried, would be right enough. No man ever really acts against what he apprehends at the time to be his interest, though his interest may lead him to sacrifice his animal or individual to his domestic or social desires.

Goldwin Smith
Guesses at the Riddle of Existence

LITTLE BY LITTLE

LITTLE by little, as some down-trod weed
    Leaf after leaf lifts painfully again,
      Does life renew its uses.   Though remain
Desire nor hope, though every heart-wound bleed,

Nature's high law no mortal may impede
    In its remorseless working.   Wholly vain
      Protest or strife ; we to obey are fain,
Slaves of strong destiny in thought and deed.

As those whom destiny compels, we take
    One after one all life's old duties up ;
Its cares and fears, its terrors and its ache ;

Even its joys, though each, an empty cup
    Where once was wine, but serves the thought to
      wake
Of draught divine we once from it did sup.

ARLO BATES
Sonnets in Shadow

SCIENCE AND MORALS

IF the diseases of society consist in the weakness of
    its faith in the existence of the God of the the-
ologians, in a future state, and in uncaused volitions,
the indication, as the doctors say, is to suppress theology and philosophy, whose bickerings about things of

Science and Morals

which they know nothing have been the prime cause and continual sustenance of that evil scepticism which is the nemesis of meddling with the unknowable.

Cinderella is modestly conscious of her ignorance of these high matters. She lights the fire, sweeps the house, and provides the dinner; and is rewarded by being told that she is a base creature, devoted to low and material interests. But in her garret she has fairy visions out of the ken of the pair of shrews who are quarreling downstairs. She sees the order which pervades the seeming disorder of the world ; the great drama of evolution, with its full share of pity and terror, but also with abundant goodness and beauty, unrolls itself before her eyes, and she learns in her heart of hearts the lesson that the foundation of morality is to have done, once and for all, with lying ; to give up pretending to believe that for which there is no evidence, and repeating unintelligible propositions about things beyond the possibilities of knowledge.

She knows that the safety of morality lies neither in the adoption of this or that philosophical speculation, or this or that philosophical creed, but in a real and living belief in that fixed order of nature which sends social disorganization upon the track of immorality as surely as it sends physical disease after physical tresspasses. And of that firm and lively faith it is her high mission to be the priestess.

THOMAS HENRY HUXLEY
Essays

ALONG THE NOISY CITY WAYS

ALONG the noisy city ways
    And in this rattling city car,
On this the dreariest of days,
    Perplexed with business fret and jar,

When suddenly a young, sweet face
    Looked on my petulance and pain
And lent it something of its grace
    And charmed it into peace again.

The day was just as bleak without,
    My neighbors just as cold within,
And truth was just as full of doubt,
    The world was just as full of sin.

But in the light of that young smile
    The world grew pure, the heart grew warm,
And sunshine gleamed a little while
    Across the darkness of the storm.

I did not care to seek her name,
    I only said, "God bless thy life,
Thy sweet young grace be still the same,
    Or happy maid or happy wife."

1858   PHILLIPS BROOKS

The above was found in one of Phillips Brooks' early note-books in which he jotted down thoughts and memoranda.—*Boston Transcript.*

THE SOUL AND THE FUTURE LIFE

THE strength of the human future over the celestial future is clearly pre-eminent. Make the future hope a social activity, and we give to the present life a social ideal. Make the future hope personal beatitude, and personality is stamped deeper on every act of our daily life. Now we may make the future hope, in the truest sense, social, inasmuch as our future is simply an active existence prolonged by society. And our future hope rests not in any vague yearning, of which we have as little evidence as we have definite conception : it rests on a perfectly certain truth accepted by all thoughtful minds, the truth that the actions, feelings, thoughts, of every one of us—our minds, our characters, our *souls*, as organic wholes—do marvelously mold and influence each other ; that the highest part of ourselves, the abiding part of us, passes into other lives, and continues to live in other lives. Can we conceive a more potent stimulus to rectitude, to daily and hourly striving after true life than this ever present sense that we are indeed immortal ; not that we have an immortal something within us, but that in very truth we ourselves, our thinking, feeling, acting personalities, are immortal; nay, cannot die, but must ever continue what we make them, working and doing, if no longer receiving and enjoying ? And not merely we ourselves, in our personal identity, are immortal, but each act, thought, and feeling is immortal, and this immortality is not

Alternatives

some ecstatic and indescribable condition in space, but activity on earth in the real and known work of life, in the welfare of those whom we have loved, and in the happiness of those who come after us.

The difference between our faith and that of the orthodox is this : we look to the permanence of the activities which give others happiness ; they look to the permanence of the consciousness which can enjoy happiness. Which is the nobler ?

FREDERIC HARRISON

See reply to above by Thomas Henry Huxley, in Section First

ALTERNATIVES

LONG fed on boundless hopes, O race of man,
  How angrily thou spurn'st all simple fare !
Christ, some one says, was human, as we are ;
No judge eyes us from heaven, our sin to scan ;
We live no more when we have done our span,
  " Well, then for Christ," thou answerest, " who can
    care ?
From sin which Heaven records not, why forbear ?
Live we like brutes our life without a plan ! "
  So answerest thou ; but why not rather say—
" Hath man no second life ?   Pitch this one high.
  Sits there no judge in heaven our sin to see ?
  More strictly, then, the inward judge obey !
Was Christ a man like us ?   Ah, let us try
  If we, too, then, can be such men as he ! "

MATTHEW ARNOLD

MAN CAN DO HIS DUTY

THE impossibility of conceiving that this grand and wondrous universe, with our conscious selves, arose through chance, seems to me the chief argument for the existence of God ; but whether this is an argument of real value, I have never been able to decide. I am aware that if we admit a first cause, the mind still craves to know whence it came, and how it arose. Nor can I overlook the difficulty from the immense amount of suffering through the world. I am, also, induced to defer to a certain extent to the judgment of the many able men who have fully believed in God ; but here again I see how poor an argument this is. The safest conclusion seems to me that the whole subject is beyond the scope of man's intellect ; but man can do his duty. CHARLES DARWIN
Life and Letters

In answer to a request for his views on religion

A FLIGHT FROM GLORY

ONCE, from the parapet of gems and glow,
    An Angel said, " O God, the heart grows cold
On these eternal battlements of gold,
Where all is pure, but cold as virgin snow.

Here sobs are never heard ; no salt tears flow ;
    Here there are none to help—nor sick nor old ;
    No wrong to fight, no justice to uphold :
Grant me thy leave to live man's life below."

Not in Vain

"And then annihilation ? " God replied.
  " Yes," said the Angel, " even that dread price ;
For earthly tears are worth eternal night."

" Then go," said God.—The Angel opened wide
  His dazzling wings, gazed back on Heaven thrice,
And plunged for ever from the walls of Light.

EUGENE LEE-HAMILTON
" *Sonnets of the Wingless Hours* "

NOT IN VAIN

LET me not deem that I was made in vain,
  Or that my being was an accident
Which Fate, in working its sublime intent,
Not wished to be, to hinder would not deign.
Each drop uncounted in a storm of rain
  Hath its own mission, and is duly sent
  To its own leaf or blade, not idly spent
'Mid myriad dimples on the shipless main.
The very shadow of an insect's wing,
  For which the violet cared not while it stayed
Yet felt the lighter for its vanishing,
  Proved that the sun was shining by its shade.
Then can a drop of the eternal spring,
  Shadow of living lights, in vain be made ?

HARTLEY COLERIDGE

MORTAL MEN MAY BE GOOD MEN

THOMAS YOUNG in "Night Thoughts" (First Night), says :

> "As in the dying parent dies the child,
> Virtue with Immortality expires.
> Who tells me he denies the soul immortal,
> Whate'er his boast, has told me he's a knave.
> His duty is to love himself alone,
> Nor care if mankind perish, if he smiles."

We can imagine the man who "denies his soul immortal," replying, "It is quite possible that *you* would be a knave, and love yourself alone, if it were not for your belief in immortality; but you are not to force upon me what would result from your own want of moral emotion. I am just and honest, not because I expect to live in another world, but because, having felt the pain of injustice and dishonesty toward myself, I have a fellow-feeling with other men, who would suffer the same pain if I were unjust or dishonest toward them. Why should I give my neighbor short weight in this world, because there is not another world in which I should have nothing to weigh out to him? I am honest because I don't like to inflict evil on others in this life, not because I am afraid of evil in another. The fact is, I do *not* love myself alone, whatever logical necessity there may be for that conclusion in your mind. I have a tender love for my wife, and children, and friends, and through that love I sympathize with like affections in other men. It is a pang to me to witness the suffering of a fellow-being,

147

and I feel his suffering the more acutely because he is *mortal*—because his life is so short, and I would have it, if possible, filled with happiness and not misery. Through my union and fellowship with the men and women I *have* seen, I feel a like, though a fainter, sympathy with those I have *not* seen ; and I am able so to live in imagination with the generations to come, that their good is not alien to me, and is a stimulus to me to labor for ends which may not benefit myself, but will benefit them. It is possible that you might prefer to 'live the brute,' to sell your country, or to slay your father, if you were not afraid of some disagreeable consequences from the criminal laws of another world ; but even if I could conceive no motive but my own worldly interest or the gratification of my animal desires, I have not observed that beastliness, treachery, and parricide, are the direct way to happiness and comfort on earth."

GEORGE ELIOT
Essay on the poet Young

WE LIVE IN DEEDS

WE live in deeds, not years ; in thoughts, not
        breaths ;
In feelings, not in figures on a dial.
We should count time by heart throbs. He most lives
Who thinks most, feels the noblest, acts the best.

Yet truth and falsehood meet in seeming, like
The falling leaf and shadow on the pool's face.

While We May

Men might be better if we better deemed
Of them.   The worst way to improve the world
Is to condemn it.   Men may overget
Delusion, not despair.

PHILIP JAMES BAILEY

Festus

WHILE WE MAY

THE hands are such dear hands;
　　They are so full.   They turn at our demands
So often.   They reach out,
With trifles scarcely thought about,
　　So many times.   They do
So very many things for me, foi you ;
　　If their fond wills mistake,
We may well bend, not break.

　　They are such fond, frail lips
　　That speak to us.   Pray, if love strips
　　Them of discretion many times,
Or if they speak too slow, or quick, such crimes
　　We may pass by, for we may see
Days not far off when these small words may be
Held not as slow, or quick, or out of place, but dear
　　Because the lips are no more here.

They are such dear familiar feet that go
Along the path with ours; feet fast, or slow;
And trying to keep pace, if they mistake,
Or tread upon some flower that we would take

While We May

Upon our breast, or bruise some reed,
Or crush poor Hope until it bleed,
   We may be mute,
  Not turning to impute
  Grave fault, for they and we
 Have such a little way to go, can be
Together such a little while along the way,
  We will be patient while we may.

   So many little faults we find :
  We see them, for not blind
Is love ; we see them, but if you and I
Perhaps remember them some by and by
      They will not be
Faults then—grave faults—to you and me,
But just odd ways, mistakes, or even less,
  Remembrances to bless.

Days change so many things—yes, hours—
We see so differently in suns and showers;
  Mistaken words to-night
May be so cherished by to-morrow's light !
  We may be patient, for we know
  There's such a little way to go.

GEORGE KLINGLE

M ORAL rules, apprehended as ideas first, and
then rigorously followed as laws, are, and
must be, for the sage only. The mass of mankind
have neither force of intellect enough to apprehend
them clearly as ideas, nor force of character enough to
follow them strictly as laws. The mass of mankind
can be carried along a course full of hardship for the
natural man, can be borne over the thousand impedi-
ments of the narrow way, only by the tide of a joyful
and bounding emotion. It is impossible to rise from
reading Epictetus or Marcus Aurelius without a sense
of constraint and melancholy, without feeling that the
burden laid upon man is well-nigh greater than he can
bear. Honor to the sages who have felt this, and yet
have borne it ! Yet, even for the sage, this sense of
labor and sorrow in his march toward the goal constitutes a relative inferiority ; the noblest souls of whatever creed, the pagan Empedocles as well as the
Christian Paul, have insisted on the necessity of an inspiration, a joyful emotion, to make man perfect. An
obscure indication of this necessity is the one drop of
truth in the ocean of verbiage with which the con-
troversy on justification by faith has flooded the world.
But, for the ordinary man, this sense of labor and
sorrow constitutes an absolute disqualification ; it par-
alyzes him ; under the weight of it he cannot make
way toward the goal at all. The paramount virtue of

Reveille

religion is, that it has *lighted up* morality ; that it has supplied the emotion and the inspiration needful for carrying the sage along the narrow way perfectly, for carrying the ordinary man along it at all. Even the religions with most dross in them have had something of this virtue ; but the Christian religion manifests it with unexampled splendor.

MATTHEW ARNOLD

Essays in Criticism

REVÉILLÉ

SLEEPERS, awake ! the night is slowly dying,
The dawn is breaking on a thousand hills,
The truth is trickling in a thousand rills,
The phantoms of the past are swiftly flying,
The idols ignominiously lying
Deep in the dust of self-deluded wills,
The legendary righteousness that fills
Our bosoms with uncertainty and sighing,
The ignorance that knows not—cares not—why ;
The cowardice that trembles at the firing,
The selfishness that truckles to a lie,
The prejudice that interdicts inquiring,
Did God give mind then but to dig a grave
Wherein to bury all the gifts He gave ?

PHILIP ACTON

RELIGION AND CONDUCT

FOR my part I do not admit that morality is not strong enough to hold its own. But if it is demonstrated to me that I am wrong, and that without this or that theological dogma the human race will lapse into bipedal cattle, more brutal than the beasts by the measure of their greater cleverness, my next question is to ask for proof of the truth of the dogma. If this proof is forthcoming, it is my conviction that no drowning sailor ever clutched a hen-coop more tenaciously than mankind will hold by such dogma, whatever it may be. But if not, then I verily believe that the human race will go its evil way ; and my only consolation lies in the reflection that, however bad our posterity may become, so long as they hold by the plain rule of not pretending to believe what they have no reason to believe because it may be to their advantage so to pretend, they will not have reached the lowest depths of immorality.

THOMAS HENRY HUXLEY

On the Influence upon Morality of a Decline in Religious
. Belief

WHEN IN DISGRACE

WHEN, in disgrace with fortune and men's eyes,
  I all alone beweep my outcast state,
And trouble deaf heaven with my bootless cries,
  And look upon myself, and curse my fate,
Wishing me like to one more rich in hope,
  Featured like him, like him with friends possess'd,
Desiring this man's art and that man's scope,
  With what I most enjoy contented least ;
Yet in these thoughts myself almost despising,
  Haply I think on thee, and then my state,
Like to the lark at break of day arising
  From sullen earth, sings hymns at heaven's gate ;
For thy sweet love remember'd such wealth brings
That then I scorn to change my state with kings.

WILLIAM SHAKSPERE

154

JOY IN THE RIGHT

EVERY age of European thought has had its Cyrenaics or Epicureans under many disguises: even under the hood of the monk. But—*Let us eat and drink, for to-morrow we die !*—is a proposal the real import of which differs immensely, according to the natural taste, and the acquired judgment, of the guests who sit at the table. It may express nothing better than the instinct of Dante's Ciacco, the accomplished glutton, in the mud of the *Inferno ;* or, since on no hypothesis does " man live by bread alone," may come to be identical with—" My meat is to do what is just and kind ; " while the soul, which can make no sincere claim to have apprehended anything beyond the veil of experience, yet never loses a sense of happiness in conforming to the highest moral ideal it can clearly define for itself ; and actually, though with but faint hope, does the " Father's business."

WALTER PATER
Marius the Epicurean

A LITTLE PARABLE

I MADE the cross myself whose weight
   Was later laid on me.
This thought is torture as I toil
   Up life's steep Calvary.

To think mine own hands drove the nails
   I sang a merry song,
And chose the heaviest wood I had
   To build it firm and strong.

If I had guessed—if I had dreamed
   Its weight was meant for me,
I should have made a lighter cross
   To bear up Calvary !

ANNE REEVE ALDRICH

Songs about Life, Love, and Death

Trust

If my bark sinks 'tis to another sea !
                    WILLIAM ELLERY CHANNING

    Rivers to the ocean run,
        Nor stay in all their course ;
    Fire ascending seeks the sun,
        Both speed them to their source
    So a soul that's born of God
        Pants to view His glorious face
    Upward tends to His abode,
        To rest in His embrace.
                        ROBERT SEAGRAVE

THE PESCADERO PEBBLES

WHERE slopes the beach to the setting sun,
   On the Pescadero shore,
For ever and ever the restless surf
  Rolls up with its sullen roar.

And grasping the pebbles in white hands,
  And chafing them together,
And grinding them against the cliffs
  In stormy and sunny weather,

It gives them never any rest:
  All day, all night, the pain
Of their long agony sobs on,
  Sinks, and then swells again.

And seekers come from every clime,
  To search with eager care,
For those whose rest has been the least;
  For such have grown more fair.

But yonder, round a point of rock,
  In a quiet, sheltered cove,
Where storm ne'er breaks, and sea ne'er comes,
  The seekers never rove.

The pebbles lie 'neath the sunny sky
  Quiet forevermore :
In dreams of everlasting peace
  They sleep upon the shore.

A Dream

But ugly, and rough, and jagged still
    Are they left by the passing years ;
For they miss the beat of the angry storms,
    And the surf that drips in tears.

The hard turmoil of the pitiless sea
    Turns the pebble to beauteous gem.
They who escape the agony
    Miss also the diadem.

MINOT JUDSON SAVAGE

A DREAM

IT seemed as if I had awakened just before daybreak, and that I stood in the midst of a vast
illimitable plain, over which deep white sand was
blown into wreaths and eddies by a slowly rising wind.
Before me and beside me, as far as my eye could see,
were graves ; they had been given up to the drifting
sand so long that their outlines were wellnigh obliter-
ated. Here and there what had been the base of a
marble headstone remained white and rounded ; and
toppling memorials of granite, defaced and illegible,
told of ages of surrender to frost and sand and gale.

I had risen from my grave. I could vaguely recognize the slanting shaft near by as the lofty obelisk
erected in my boyhood to the memory of my father's
father—a man in his day eminent in the place of his

birth and death. It was the resurrection morn; I was of the first to rise from the dead. I felt no fear, only a certain benumbed expectancy. I knew that my father and mother stood behind me, but I dared not obey my strong impulse to turn and look upon them; I was restrained, I knew not why or how. In the East, from moment to moment, the morning light grew brighter; soon the sun appeared above the horizon, surely larger, more radiant than ever before. On the right hand and on the left the dead continued to come forth from the beating sand, to stand silently and calmly facing the East. Near me arose a young woman—no other than a sister who had died when I was twelve. By her side stood her little daughter. Then appeared her husband, who had died in middle life, and last of all an old man with shriveled front and long white hair; he exchanged glances with my sister, and I knew that she, the young woman, was mother to this old man.

Little by little the plain throughout its whole expanse became thickly peopled. In all that vast multitude nearly every face was peaceful; only a few bore marks of the pain which had been their last pain, and gradually these traces faded away. Men and women, youths and maidens, children and babes, all stood together with wistful gaze fixed upon the East, whence should come HE who would open the gates of the New Life. Every heart in all those myriads throbbed as did mine, there was no spirit of dread in any—only a confidence that all was well—that more and better was in store for us all than we had ever hoped or pictured; that there had been a divine inevitableness in the good and evil of that Old Life—now so far off and so much softened in the recollection.

I remember no more.

ANTOINE LEBRUN

INTIMATIONS OF IMMORTALITY

OUR birth is but a sleep and a forgetting;
The soul that rises with us, our life's star,
Hath had elsewhere its setting,
And cometh from afar,
Not in entire forgetfulness,
And not in utter nakedness,
But trailing clouds of glory do we come
From God, who is our home.
Heaven lies about us in our infancy!
Shades of the prison-house begin to close
Upon the growing boy;
But he beholds the light, and whence it flows—
He sees it in his joy.
The youth, who daily farther from the east
Must travel, still is nature's priest,
And by the vision splendid
Is on his way attended;
At length the man perceives it die away,
And fade into the light of common day.

Intimations of Immortality

Oh joy ! that in our embers
 Is something that doth live,
That nature yet remembers
 What was so fugitive !
The thought of our past years in me doth breed
Perpetual benediction : not, indeed,
 For that which is most worthy to be blest—
Delight and liberty, the simple creed
 Of childhood, whether busy or at rest,
 With new-pledged hope still fluttering in his
  breast—
 Not for these I raise
 The song of thanks and praise ;
 But for those obstinate questionings
 Of sense and outward things,
 Fallings from us, vanishings,
 Blank misgivings of a creature
Moving about in worlds not realized,
 High instincts, before which our mortal nature
Did tremble like a guilty thing surprised—
 But for those first affections,
 Those shadowy recollections,
 Which, be they what they may,
 Are yet the fountain-light of all our day,
Are yet a master light of all our seeing,
 Uphold us, cherish, and have power to make
Our noisy years seem moments in the being
 Of the eternal silence : truths to wake,
  To perish never—
Which neither listlessness, nor mad endeavor,

Interlacements

Nor man, nor boy,
Nor all that is at enmity with joy,
Can utterly abolish or destroy !
Hence in a season of calm weather,
Though inland far we be,
Our souls have sight of that immortal sea
Which brought us hither—
Can in a moment travel thither;
And see the children sport upon the shore,
And hear the mighty waters rolling evermore.

WILLIAM WORDSWORTH

INTERLACEMENTS

IN human works, though labored on with pain,
A thousand movements scarce one purpose gain ;
With God's, a single can its end produce,
Yet serves to second, too, some other use.
So man, who here seems principal alone,
Perhaps acts second to some sphere unknown,
Touches some wheel, or verges to some goal,
'Tis but a part we see, and not the whole.

ALEXANDER POPE
Essay on Man

I CONFESS that I do not see why the very existence of an invisible world may not in part depend on the personal response which any one of us may make to the religious appeal. God, himself, in short, may draw vital strength and increase of very being from our fidelity. For my part, I do not know what the sweat and blood and tragedy of this life mean, if they mean anything short of this. If this life be not a real fight, in which something is eternally gained for the universe by success, it is no better than a game of private theatricals from which one may withdraw at will. But it *feels* like a real fight—as if there were something really wild in the universe which we, with all our idealities and faithfulnesses, were needed to redeem ; and first of all to redeem our own hearts from atheisms and fears. For such a half-wild, half-saved universe our nature is adapted. The deepest thing in our nature is this dumb region of the heart in which we dwell alone with our willingnesses and unwillingnesses, our faiths and fears. As through the cracks and crannies of caverns those waters exude from the earth's bosom which then form the fountain-heads of springs, so in these crepuscular depths of personality the sources of all our outer deeds and decisions take their rise. Here is our deepest organ of communication with the nature of things; and compared with these concrete movements of our soul all abstract

Is Life Worth Living ?

statements and scientific arguments—the veto, for example, which the positivist pronounces upon our faith —sound to us like mere chatterings of the teeth. For here possibilities, not finished facts, are the realities with which we have actively to deal; and to quote William Salter, "as the essence of courage is to stake one's life on a possibility, so the essence of faith is to believe that the possibility exists."

These, then, are my last words to you : Be not afraid of life. Believe that life *is* worth living, and your belief will help create the fact. The "scientific proof" that you are right may not be clear before the day of judgment (or some stage of being which that expression may serve to symbolize) is reached. But the faithful fighters of this hour, or the beings that then and there will represent them, may then turn to the faint-hearted, who here decline to go on, with words like those which Henry IV. greeted the tardy Crillon after a great victory had been gained : "Hang yourself, brave Crillon ! we fought at Arques, and you were not there."

WILLIAM JAMES
The Will to Believe

HOPE

WE cannot know
     Aught of that far-off realm by us named
          heaven,
Where, in our fancy, lilies pure as snow
Fleck all the emerald meadows which are riven
     By wondrous singing streams. We cannot know
          Until we go.

We may not tell
If our freed spirit, searching, shall discover
     The kindred souls of those we loved so well,
Who, when they passed death's midnight river over,
     Passed speechless and alone. We may not tell
          Nor yet rebel.

Have we not left
That grand impulse to every great endeavor,
     Which swathes the broken heart by partings cleft ?
Hope, skyward, burns its beacon-light forever,
     Beckoning us toward the truth : this we have left
          Who are bereft.

UNKNOWN
The Radical, Boston, November, 1868

Reply to "The Undiscovered Country," by Edmund Clarence Stedman ; see Section First.

167

THE IDEA OF GOD

THE infinite and eternal Power that is manifested in every pulsation of the universe is none other than the living God. We may exhaust the resources of metaphysics in debating how far his nature may fitly be expressed in terms applicable to the psychical nature of Man ; such vain attempts will only serve to show how we are dealing with a theme that must ever transcend our finite powers of conception. But of some things we may feel sure. Humanity is not a mere local incident in an endless and aimless series of cosmical changes. The events of the universe are not the work of chance, neither are they the outcome of blind necessity. Practically there is a purpose in the world whereof it is our highest duty to learn the lesson, however well or ill we may fare in rendering a scientific account of it. When from the dawn of life we see things working together toward the evolution of the highest spiritual attributes of Man, we know, however the words may stumble in which we try to say it, that God is in the deepest sense a moral Being. The everlasting source of phenomena is none other than the infinite Power that makes for Righteousness. Thou canst not by searching find Him out ; yet put thy trust in Him, and against thee the gates of hell shall not prevail ; for there is neither wisdom nor understanding nor counsel against the Eternal.

JOHN FISKE
The Idea of God

WAITING

SERENE I fold my hands and wait,
   Nor care for wind, or tide, or sea ;
I rave no more 'gainst time or fate,
   For lo ! my own shall come to me.

I stay my haste, I make delays,
   For what avails this eager pace ?
I stand amid the eternal ways,
   And what is mine shall know my face.

Asleep, awake, by night or day,
   The friends I seek are seeking me ;
No wind can drive my bark astray,
   Nor change the tide of destiny.

What matter if I stand alone ?
   I wait with joy the coming years ;
My heart shall reap where it has sown,
   And garner up its fruit of tears.

The waters know their own, and draw
   The brook that springs in yonder heights ;
So flows the good with equal law
   Unto the soul of pure delights.

The stars come nightly to the sky,
   The tidal wave unto the sea ;
Nor time, nor space, nor deep, nor high,
   Can keep my own away from me.

JOHN BURROUGHS

REASON

DIM as the borrow'd beams of moon and stars
  To lonely, weary, wandering travelers,
Is Reason to the soul ; and as on high
Those rolling fires discover but the sky,
Not light us here ; so Reason's glimmering ray
Was lent, not to assure our doubtful way
But guide us upward to a better day,
And as those nightly tapers disappear,
When day's bright lord ascends our hemisphere ;
So pale grows Reason at Religion's sight ;
So dies, and so dissolves, in supernatural light.

JOHN DRYDEN
Religio Laici

SEEN AND UNSEEN

OH, thou God's mariner, heart of mine,
  Spread canvas to the airs divine !
Spread sail ! and let thy fortune be
Forgotten in thy Destiny.

For Destiny pursues us well,
By sea, by land, through heaven or hell :
It suffers Death alone to die,
Bids Life all change and chance defy.

Seen and Unseen

Would earth's dark ocean suck thee down ?
Earth's ocean thou, O Life, shalt drown,
Shalt flood it with thy finer wave,
And, sepulchered, entomb thy grave !

Life loveth life and good ; then trust
What most the spirit would, it must ;
Deep wishes, in the heart that be,
Are blossoms of Necessity.

A thread of law runs through thy prayer,
Stronger than iron cables are ;
And Love and Longing toward her goal
Are pilots sweet to guide the Soul.

So Life must live, and Soul must sail,
And Unseen over Seen prevail,
And all God's argosies come to shore,
Let ocean smile, or rage or roar.

And so, 'mid storm or calm, my bark
With snowy wake still nears her mark ;
Cheerily the trades of being blow,
And sweeping down the wind I go.

DAVID ATWOOD WASSON

"I VEX ME NOT WITH BROODING ON THE YEARS"

I VEX me not with brooding on the years
  That were ere I drew breath : why should I then
Distrust the darkness that may fall again
When life is done ?   Perchance in other spheres—
Dead planets—I once tasted mortal tears,
  And walked as now among a throng of men,
  Pondering things that lay beyond my ken,
Questioning death, and solacing my fears.
Who knows ?   Ofttimes strange sense have I of this,
  Vague memories that hold me with a spell,
  Touches of unseen lips upon my brow,
Breathing some incommunicable bliss !
  In years foregone, O Soul, was all not well ?
  Still lovelier life awaits thee.   Fear not thou !

THOMAS BAILEY ALDRICH

O THOU, WHOSE IMAGE

O THOU, whose image in the shrine
  Of human spirits dwells divine.
Which from that precinct once conveyed,
To be to outer day displayed,
Doth vanish, part, and leave behind
Mere blank and void of empty mind,
Which willful fancy seeks in vain
With casual shapes to fill again.

The Larger Prayer

O Thou, that in our bosom's shrine
Dost dwell, unknown because divine.
I thought to speak, I thought to say,
"The light is here," "Behold the way,"
"The voice was thus," and "Thus the word,"
And "Thus I saw," and "That I heard";
But from the lips that half essayed,
The imperfect utterance fell unmade.

O Thou, in that mysterious shrine
Enthroned, as I must say, divine.
I will not frame one thought of what
Thou mayst either be or not.
I will not prate of "thus" and "so,"
And be profane with "yes" and "no":
Enough that in our soul and heart
Thou, whatso'er Thou mayest be, art.

ARTHUR HUGH CLOUGH

THE LARGER PRAYER

AT first I prayed for Light :
    Could I but see the way,
How gladly, swiftly would I walk
    To everlasting day !

And next I prayed for Strength :
    That I might tread the road
With firm unfaltering feet, and win
    The heaven's serene abode.

Blessed Are They That Mourn

And then I asked for Faith :
  Could I but trust my God,
I'd live enfolded in his peace,
  Though foes were all abroad.

But now I pray for Love :
  Deep love to God and man,
A living love that will not fail,
  However dark his plan.

And Light and Strength and Faith
  Are opening everywhere !
God only waited for me till
  I prayed the larger prayer.

EDNAH DOW CHENEY.

BLESSED ARE THEY THAT MOURN

O DEEM not that earth's crowning bliss
  Is found in joy alone ;
For sorrow, bitter though it be,
  Hath blessings all its own.

From lips divine, like healing balm
  To hearts oppressed and torn,
The heavenly consolation fell,—
  "Blessed are they that mourn."

Prayer of a Deaf and Dumb Boy

Who never mourn'd hath never known
    What treasures grief reveals,
The sympathies that humanize,
    The tenderness that heals.

The power to look within the veil,
    And learn the heavenly lore,
The key-word to life's mysteries,
    So dark to us before.

Supernal wisdom, love divine,
    Breathed thro' the lips which said,
" O blessed are the souls that mourn,
    They shall be comforted."

WILLIAM HENRY BURLEIGH

PRAYER OF A DEAF AND DUMB BOY

"WHEN my long attached friend comes to me, I have pleasure to converse with him, and I rejoice to pass my eyes over his countenance ; but soon I weary of spending my time causelessly and un-improved, and I desire to leave him (but not in rudeness), because I wished to be engaged in my business. But thou, O my Father, knowest I always delight to commune with thee in my lone and silent heart ; I am never full of thee ; I am always desiring thee. I hunger with strong hope and affection for thee, and I thirst for thy grace and thy spirit.

Let Down the Bars, O Death!

"When I go to visit my friends, I must put on my best garments, and I must think of my manner to please them. I am tired to stay long, because my mind is not free, and they sometimes talk gossip with me. But oh, my Father, thou visitest me in my work, and I can lift up my desires to thee, and thou dost not steal my time by foolishness. I always ask in my heart, where can I find thee?"

Quoted by Ralph Waldo Emerson in an Essay on
Prayer

LET DOWN THE BARS, O DEATH!

LET down the bars, O Death!
　　The tired flocks come in
Whose bleating ceases to repeat,
Whose wandering is done.

Thine is the stillest night,
Thine the securest fold;
Too near thou art for seeking thee,
Too tender to be told.

A death-blow is a life-blow to some
Who, till they died, did not alive become;
Who, had they lived, had died, but when
They died, vitality begun.

EMILY DICKINSON

COME NOT, OH LORD!

COME not, oh Lord! in the dread robe of
    splendor
Thou worest on the Mount, in the day of Thine ire;
Come veiled in those shadows, deep, awful, but tender,
    Which Mercy flings over Thy features of fire!

Lord! Thou rememberest the night when Thy nation
    Stood fronting her foe by the red-rolling stream;
On Egypt Thy pillar frowned dark desolation,
    While Israel basked all the night in its beam.

So when the dread clouds of anger enfold Thee,
    From us, in Thy mercy, the dark side remove;
While shrouded in terrors the guilty behold Thee,
    Oh, turn upon us the mild light of Thy Love!

THOMAS MOORE.

EVELYN HOPE

BEAUTIFUL Evelyn Hope is dead!
    Sit and watch by her side an hour.
That is her book-shelf, this her bed;
    She plucked that piece of geranium-flower,
Beginning to die, too, in the glass;
    Little has yet been changed, I think:
The shutters are shut—no light may pass,
    Save two long rays thro' the hinge's chink.

Evelyn Hope

Sixteen years old when she died !
    Perhaps she had scarcely heard my name ;
It was not her time to love : beside,
    Her life had many a hope and aim
Duties enough and little cares,
    And now was quiet, now astir,
Till God's hand beckoned unawares,—
    And the sweet white brow is all of her.

Is it too late, then, Evelyn Hope ?
    What ! your soul was pure and true ;
The good stars met in your horoscope,
    Made you of spirit, fire, and dew—
And, just because I was thrice as old,
    And our paths in the world diverged so wide,
Each was nought to each, must I be told ?
We were fellow-mortals—nought beside ?

No, indeed ! for God above
    Is great to grant, as mighty to make,
And creates the love to reward the love ;
    I claim you still, for my own love's sake !
Delayed, it may be for more lives yet,
    Through worlds I shall traverse, not a few ;
Much is to learn, and much to forget
    Ere the time be come for taking you.

Evelyn Hope

But the time will come—at last it will,
   When, Evelyn Hope, what meant, (I shall say,)
In the lower earth, in the years long still—
   That body and soul so pure and gay?
Why your hair was amber, I shall divine,
   And your mouth of your own geranium's red,
And what you would do with me, in fine,
   In the new life come in the old one's stead.

I have lived, (I shall say) so much since then,
   Given up myself so many times,
Gained me the gains of various men,
   Ransacked the ages, spoiled the climes;
Yet one thing—one—in my soul's full scope,
   Either I missed or itself missed me:
And I want to find you, Evelyn Hope!
   What is the issue? Let us see!

I loved you, Evelyn, all the while.
   My heart seemed full as it could hold?
There was place and to spare for the frank young
     smile,
   And the red young mouth, and the hair's young
     gold.
So, hush,—I will give you this leaf to keep;
   See, I shut it inside the sweet, cold hand!
There, that is our secret! go to sleep!
   You will wake, and remember, and understand.

                   ROBERT BROWNING.

THE PULLEY

WHEN God at first made man,
    Having a glass of blessings standing by,
Let us, said He, pour on him all we can,
    Let the world's riches, which dispersed lie,
Contract into a span.

So strength first made a way,
    Then beauty flowed, then wisdom, honor, pleasure;
When almost all was out God made a stay,
    Perceiving that alone of all His treasure
Rest at the bottom lay.

For if I should, said He,
    Bestow this jewel also on my creature,
He would adore my gifts instead of me,
    And rest in nature, not the God of nature,
So both should losers be.

Yet let him keep the rest,
    But keep them with repining restlessness;
Let him be rich and weary, that at least
    If goodness lead him not, yet weariness
May toss him to my breast.

GEORGE HERBERT

I GRIEVE NOT

I GRIEVE not that ripe Knowledge takes away
   The charm that Nature to my childhood wore,
For, with that insight, cometh day by day,
   A greater bliss than wonder was before ;
The real doth not clip the poet's wings,—
   To win the secret of a weed's plain heart
Reveals some clew to spiritual things,
   And stumbling guess becomes firm-footed art :
Flowers are not flowers unto the poet's eyes,
   Their beauty thrills him with an inward sense ;
He knows that outward seemings are but lies,
   Or, at the most, but earthly shadows, whence
The soul that looks within for truth may guess
The presence of some wondrous heavenliness.

JAMES RUSSELL LOWELL

IMMORTALITY

FOR my own part, therefore, I believe in the immortality of the soul, not in the sense in which
I accept the demonstrable truths of science, but as a
supreme act of faith in the reasonableness of God's
work. Such a belief, relating to regions quite inac-
cessible to experience, cannot, of course, be clothed in
terms of definite and tangible meaning. For the experience which alone can give us such terms we must
await that solemn day which is to overtake us all.

Immortality

The belief can be most quickly defined by its negation, as the refusal to believe that this world is all. The materialist holds that when you have described the whole universe of phenomena, of which we can become cognizant under the conditions of the present life, then the whole story is told. It seems to me, on the contrary, that the whole story is not told. I feel the omnipresence of mystery in such wise as to make it far easier for me to adopt the view of Euripides, that what we call death may be but the dawning of true knowledge and true life. The greatest philosopher of modern times, the master and teacher of all who shall study the process of evolution for many a day to come, holds that the conscious soul is not the product of a collocation of material particles, but is, in the deepest sense, a divine effluence. According to Mr. Spencer, the divine energy which is manifested throughout the knowable universe is the same energy that wells up in us as consciousness. Speaking for myself, I can see no insuperable difficulty in the notion that at some period in the evolution of Humanity this divine spark may have acquired sufficient concentration and steadiness to survive the wreck of material forms and endure forever. Such a crowning wonder seems to me no more than the fit climax to a creative work that has been ineffably beautiful and marvelous in all its myriad stages. JOHN FISKE
The Destiny of Man

IO VICTIS

I SING the hymn of the conquered, who fell in the
    battle of life—
The hymn of the wounded, the beaten, who died over-
    whelmed in the strife ;
Not the jubilant song of the victors, for whom the
    resounding acclaim
Of nations was lifted in chorus, whose brows wore the
    chaplet of fame,
But the hymn of the low and the humble, the weary,
    the broken in heart,
Who strove and who failed, acting bravely a silent and
    desperate part ;
Whose youth had no flower in its branches, whose hopes
    burned in ashes away,
From whose hands slipped the prize they had grasped
    at, who stood at the dying of day
With the wreck of their life all around them, unpitied,
    unheeded, alone,
With death swooping down o'er their failure, and all
    but their faith overthrown.

While the voice of the world shouts its chorus—its
    pæan for those who have won ;
While the trumpet is sounding triumphant, and high
    to the breeze and the sun

Io Victis

Gay banners are waving, hands clapping, and hurrying
    feet
Thronging after the laurel-crowned victors, I stand on
    the field of defeat,
In the shadow, with those who are fallen, and wounded,
    and dying, and there
Chant a requiem low, place my hand on their pain-
    knotted brows, breathe a prayer,
Hold the hand that is helpless, and whisper, "They
    only the victory win,
Who have fought the good fight, and have vanquished
    the demon that tempts us within ;
Who have held to their faith, unseduced by the prize
    that the world holds on high ;
Who have dared for a high cause to suffer, resist, fight
    —if need be, to die."

Speak, History ! Who are Life's victors ? Unroll
    thy long annals, and say,
Are they those whom the world called the victors—
    who won the success of a day ?
The martyrs, or Nero ? The Spartans, who fell at
    Thermopylæ's tryst,
Or the Persians and Xerxes ? His judges, or Socrates?
    Pilate, or Christ ?

William Wetmore Story

SONG OF THE MYSTIC

I WALK down the Valley of Silence—
  Down the dim voiceless Valley—alone !
And I hear not the fall of a footstep
  Around me, save God's and my own ;
And the hush of my heart is as holy
  As hovers where angels have flown !

Long ago was I weary of voices
  Whose music my heart could not win ;
Long ago was I weary of noises
  That fretted my soul with their din ;
Long ago was I weary of places
  Where I met but the human—and sin.

I walked through the world with the worldly ;
  I craved what the world never gave ;
And I said : " In the world, each Ideal
  That shines like a star on life's wave,
Is wrecked on the shores of the Real,
  And sleeps like a dream in a grave."

And still did I pine for the Perfect,
  And still found the false with the true ;
I sought 'mid the human for heaven,
  And caught a mere glimpse of its blue ;
And I wept when the clouds of the mortal
  Veiled even that glimpse from my view.

Song of the Mystic

And I toiled on, heart-tired of the Human ;
   And I moaned 'mid the mazes of men ;
Till I knelt, long ago, at an altar
   And heard a voice call me.   Since then
I walk down the Valley of Silence
   That lies far beyond human ken.

Do you ask what I found in the Valley ?
   'Tis my trysting-place with the Divine ;
And I fell at the feet of the Holy,
   And above me, a voice said : " Be mine ! "
And there arose from the depths of my spirit
   An echo—" My heart shall be thine."

Do you ask how I live in the Valley ?
   I weep—and I dream—and I pray.
But my tears are as sweet as the dew drops
   That fall on the roses in May ;
And my prayer, like a perfume from censers,
   Ascendeth to God, night and day.

In the hush of the Valley of Silence,
   I dream all the songs that I sing ;
And the music floats down the dim Valley,
   Till each finds a word for a wing,
That to men, like the Dove of the Deluge,
   A message of Peace they may bring.

But far on the deep there are billows
   That never shall break on the beach ;
And I have heard songs in the Silence

The Future

That never shall float into speech ;
And I have had dreams in the Valley
  Too lofty for language to reach.

And I have seen Thoughts in the Valley—
  Ah, me ! how my spirit was stirred !
And they wear holy veils on their faces,
  Their footsteps can scarcely be heard ;
They pass through the Valley, like virgins
  Too pure for the touch of a word !

Do you ask me the place of the Valley,
  Ye hearts that are harrowed by Care ?
It lieth afar, between mountains,
  And God and His angels are there ;
And one is the dark mount of Sorrow,
  And one the bright mountain of Prayer.

                        REV. ABRAM J. RYAN

THE FUTURE

WHAT may we take into the vast Forever ?
          That marble door
Admits no fruit of all our long endeavor,
          No fame-wreathed crown we wore,
          No garnered lore.

The Future

What can we bear beyond the unknown portal ?
    No gold, no gains,
Of all our toiling : in the life immortal
    No hoarded wealth remains,
    Nor gilds, nor stains.

Naked from out that far abyss behind us
    We entered here :
No word came with our coming, to remind us
    What wondrous world vas near,
    No hope, no fear.

Into the silent, starless Night before us,
    Naked we glide :
No hand has mapped the constellations o'er us,
    No comrade at our side,
    No chart, no guide.

Yet fearless toward that midnight, black and hollow,
    Our footsteps fare ;
The beckoning of a Father's hand we follow—
    His love alone is there,
    No curse, no care.

EDWARD ROWLAND SILL

CHRISTIANITY WILL SURVIVE

CHRISTIANITY will survive because of its natural truth. Those who fancied they had done with it, those who had thrown it aside because what was presented under its name was so unreceivable, will have to return to it again, and to learn it better. The Latin nations—even the Southern Latin nations—will have to acquaint themselves with that fundamental document of Christianity, the Bible, and to discover wherein it differs from " a text of Hesiod." Neither will the old forms of Christian worship be extinguished by the growth of a truer conception of their essential contents. Those forms thrown out at dimly grasped truth, approximate and provisional representations of it, and which are now surrounded with such an atmosphere of tender and profound sentiment, will not disappear. They will survive as poetry. Above all, among the Catholic nations will this be the case. And, indeed, one must wonder at the fatuity of the Roman Catholic Church, that she should not herself see what a future there is for her here. Will there never arise among Catholics some great soul, to perceive that the eternity and universality, which is vainly claimed for Catholic dogma and the ultramontane system, might really be possible for Catholic worship ? But to rule over the moment and the credulous has more attraction than to work for the future and the sane.

MATTHEW ARNOLD

Essays

THE CHAMBERED NAUTILUS

THIS is the ship of pearl, which, poets feign,
 Sails the unshadowed main,—
 The venturous bark that flings
On the sweet summer wind its purpled wings
In gulfs enchanted, where the siren sings,
 And coral reefs lie bare,
Where the cold sea-maids rise to sun their streaming
  hair.

Its webs of living gauze no more unfurl ;
 Wrecked is the ship of pearl !
 And every chambered cell,
Where its dim, dreaming life was wont to dwell,
As the frail tenant shaped his growing shell,
 Before thee lies revealed,
Its irised ceiling rent, its sunless crypt unsealed !

Year after year beheld the silent toil
 That spread his lustrous coil ;
 Still, as the spiral grew,
He left the past year's dwelling for the new,
Stole with soft step its shining archway through,
 Built up its idle door,
Stretched in his last-found home, and knew the old no
  more.

Under the Leaves

Thanks for the heavenly message brought by thee,
    Child of the wandering sea,
    Cast from her lap forlorn !
From thy dead lips a clearer note is born
Than ever Triton blew from wreathèd horn !
    While on mine ear it rings,
Through the deep caves of thought I hear the voice
      that sings :

Build thee more stately mansions, O my soul,
    As the swift seasons roll !
    Leave thy low-vaulted past !
Let each new temple, nobler than the last,
Shut thee from heaven with a dome more vast,
    Till thou at length art free,
Leaving thine outgrown shell by life's unresting sea !
OLIVER WENDELL HOLMES

UNDER THE LEAVES

OFT have I walked these woodland paths
    In sadness, not foreknowing
That underneath the withered leaves
    The flowers of Spring were growing.

To-day the winds have swept away
    Those wrecks of Autumn splendor,
And here the sweet Arbutus flowers
    Are springing, fresh and tender.

On His Blindness

O prophet flowers ! with lips of bloom
   Surpassing in their beauty
The pearly tints of ocean-shells—
   Ye teach me faith and duty.

" Walk life's dark ways," ye seem to say,
   " In love and hope, foreknowing
That where man sees but withered leaves
   God sees the sweet flowers growing ! "
ALBERT LAIGHTON.

ON HIS BLINDNESS

WHEN I consider how my light is spent
   Ere half my days, in this dark world and
wide,
And that one talent which is death to hide
Lodged with me useless, though my soul more bent
To serve therewith my Maker, and present
   My true account, lest he returning chide—
   " Doth God exact day-labor, light denied ? "
I fondly ask ; but patience, to prevent
That murmur, soon replies : " God doth not need
   Either man's work, or his own gifts ; who best
     Bear his mild yoke, they serve him best ; his state
Is kingly ; thousands at his bidding speed,
   And post o'er land and ocean without rest ;
     They also serve who only stand and wait."
JOHN MILTON

NIGHT AND DEATH

MYSTERIOUS Night! when our first parent knew
Thee by report divine, and heard thy name,
Did he not tremble for this lovely frame
This glorious canopy of light and blue ?
Yet, 'neath a curtain of translucent dew,
Bathed in the rays of the great setting flame,
Hesperus with the host of heaven came,
And lo ! creation widened on man's view.
Who could have thought such darkness lay concealed
Within thy beams, O Sun ! or who could find,
Whilst flow'r and leaf, and insect stood revealed,
That to such countless orbs thou mad'st us blind !
Why do we, then, shun Death with anxious strife ?—
If Light can thus deceive, wherefore not Life ?

JOSEPH BLANCO WHITE

DOUBT ITSELF IS A DECISION

IF this really be a moral universe; if by my acts I be
a factor of its destinies; if to believe where I
may doubt be itself a moral act analogous to voting
for a side not yet sure to win,—by what right shall
they close in upon me and steadily negate the deepest
conceivable function of my being by their preposterous
command that I shall stir neither hand nor foot, but
remain balancing myself in eternal and insoluble

Doubt Itself is a Decision

doubt ?   Why, doubt itself is a decision of the widest practical reach, if only because we may miss by doubting what goods we might be gaining by espousing the winning side.   But more than that ! it is often practically impossible to distinguish doubt from dogmatic negation.   If I refuse to stop a murder because I am in doubt whether it be not justifiable homicide, I am virtually abetting the crime.   If I refuse to bale out a boat because I am in doubt whether my efforts will keep her afloat, I am really helping to sink her.   If in the mountain precipice I doubt my right to risk a leap, I actively connive at my destruction.   He who commands himself not to be credulous of God, of duty, of freedom, of immortality, may again and again be indistinguishable from him who dogmatically denies them.   Scepticism in moral matters is an active ally of immorality.   Who is not for is against.   The universe will have no neutrals in these questions.   In theory as in practice, dodge or hedge, or talk as we like about a wise scepticism, we are really doing volunteer military service for one side or the other.

WILLIAM JAMES
The Will to Believe

THE ANCIENT FAITH

TRUE, the harsh founders of thy church reviled
    That ancient faith, the trust of Erin's child ;
Must thou be raking in the crumbled past
For racks and fagots in her teeth to cast ?
See from the ashes of Helvetia's pile
The whitened skull of old Servetus smile !
    Round her young heart thy "Roman Upas " threw
    Its firm, deep fibers, strengthening as she grew ;
Thy sneering voice may call them " Popish tricks,"
Her Latin prayers, her dangling crucifix,
    But *De Profundis* blessed her father's grave,
    That "idol " cross her dying mother gave !
What if some angel looks with equal eyes
On her and thee, the simple and the wise,
    Writes each dark fault against thy brighter creed,
    And drops a tear with every foolish bead !
Grieve, as thou must, o'er history's reeking page ;
Blush for the wrongs that stain thy happier age ;
    Strive with the wanderer from the better path,
    Bearing thy message meekly, not in wrath ;
Weep for the frail that err, the weak that fall,
Have thine own faith,—but hope and pray for all !

              OLIVER WENDELL HOLMES
                 A Rhymed Lesson

THE PRESENT

WE live not in our moments or our years—
    The Present we fling from us like the rind
Of some sweet Future, which we after find
Bitter to taste, or bind that in with fears,
And water it beforehand with our tears—
Vain tears for that which never may arrive :
Meanwhile the joy whereby we ought to live,
Neglected or unheeded, disappears.
Wiser it were to welcome and make ours
Whate'er of good, though small, the present brings—
Kind greetings, sunshine, songs of birds, and flowers,
With a child's pure delight in little things ;
    And of the griefs unborn to rest secure,
    Knowing that mercy ever will endure.
               RICHARD CHENEVIX TRENCH

THE FISHER'S BOY

MY life is like a stroll upon the beach
    As near the water's edge as I can go ;
My tardy steps sometimes its waves o'erreach,
    Sometimes I stay to let them overflow.

My sole employment is and scrupulous care,
    To place my gains beyond the reach of tides ;
Each smoother pebble and each shell more rare,
    Which ocean kindly to my hand confides.

Man

I have but few companions on the shore,
    They scorn the strand who sail upon the sea ;
Yet oft I think the ocean they've sailed o'er
    Is deeper known upon the strand to me.

The middle sea contains no crimson dulse,
    Its deeper waves cast up no pearls to view ;
Along the shore my hand is on its pulse,
    And I converse with many a shipwreck'd crew.
                   HENRY DAVID THOREAU

MAN

MAN is all symmetry—
    Full of proportions, one limb to another,
And all to all the world besides.
Each part may call the farthest brother;
For head with foot hath private amity,
    And both with moons and tides.

Nothing hath got so far
But man hath caught and kept it as his prey.
    His eyes dismount the highest star;
    He is in little all the sphere.
Herbs gladly heal our flesh, because that they
    Find their acquaintance there.

Man

For us the winds do blow,
The earth doth rest, heaven move, and fountains flow.
Nothing we see but means our good,
As our delight, or as our treasure;
The whole is either our cupboard of food
Or cabinet of pleasure.

The stars have us to bed—
Night draws the curtain, which the sun withdraws.
Music and light attend our head;
All things unto our flesh are kind
In their descent and being—to our mind
In their ascent and cause.

More servants wait on man
Than he'll take notice of.   In every path
He treads down that which doth befriend him
When sickness makes him pale and wan.
O mighty love!   Man is one world, and hath
Another to attend him.

Since then, my God, thou hast
So brave a palace built, oh dwell in it,
That it may dwell with thee at last !
Till then afford us so much wit
That, as the world serves us, we may serve thee,
And both thy servants be.

GEORGE HERBERT

O LORD! THAT SEEST FROM YON STARRY HEIGHT

O LORD! that seest from yon starry height
    Centered in one the future and the past,
Fashioned in thine own image, see how fast
The world obscures in me what once was bright!
Eternal Sun! the warmth which thou hast given
To cheer life's flowery April fast decays;
Yet in the hoary winter of my days
Forever green shall be my trust in Heaven.
Celestial King! O, let thy presence pass
Before my spirit, and an image fair
Shall meet that look of mercy from on high,
As the reflected image in a glass
Doth meet the look of him who seeks it there,
And owes its being to the gazer's eye.

FRANCISCO DE ALDANA
Translated by Henry W. Longfellow

TO A WATERFOWL

WHITHER, midst falling dew,
    While glow the heavens with the last steps
  of day
Far, through their rosy depths, dost thou pursue
    Thy solitary way?

To a Waterfowl

Vainly the fowler's eye
Might mark thy distant flight to do thee wrong,
As, darkly painted on the crimson sky,
Thy figure floats along.

Seek'st thou the plashy brink
Of weedy lake, or marge of river wide,
Or where the rocking billows rise and sink
On the chafed ocean side ?

There is a power whose care
Teaches thy way along the pathless coast,—
The desert and illimitable air,—
Lone wandering, but not lost.

All day thy wings have fanned,
At that far height, the cold, thin atmosphere,
Yet stoop not, weary, to the welcome land,
Though the dark night is near.

And soon that toil shall end ;
Soon shalt thou find thy summer home, and rest,
And scream among thy fellows ; reeds shall bend,
Soon, o'er thy sheltered nest.

Thou'rt gone, the abyss of heaven
Hath swallowed up thy form ; yet, on my heart
Deeply hath sunk the lesson thou hast given,
And shall not soon depart.

Through Peace to Light

He who, from zone to zone,
Guides through the boundless sky thy certain flight,
In the long way that I must tread alone,
Will lead my steps aright.

WILLIAM CULLEN BRYANT

THROUGH PEACE TO LIGHT

I DO not ask, O Lord, that life may be
A pleasant road ;
I do not ask that Thou wouldst take from me
Aught of its load ;

I do not ask that flowers should always spring
Beneath my feet ;
I know too well the poison and the sting
Of things too sweet.

For one thing only, Lord, dear Lord, I plead,
Lead me aright—
Though strength should falter, and though heart should
bleed—
Through Peace to Light.

I do not ask, O Lord, that Thou shouldst shed
Full radiance here ;
Give but a ray of peace, that I may tread
Without a fear.

The Master's Touch

I do not ask my cross to understand,
    My way to see ;
Better in darkness just to feel Thy Hand
    And follow Thee.

Joy is like restless day ; but peace divine
    Like quiet night :
Lead me, O Lord,—till perfect Day shall shine,
    Through Peace to Light.
                ADELAIDE ANNE PROCTER

THE MASTER'S TOUCH

IN the still air the music lies unheard ;
    In the rough marble beauty lies unseen ;
To wake the music and the beauty needs
    The master's touch, the sculptor's chisel keen.

Great Master, touch us with Thy skillful hand,
    Let not the music that is in us die ;
Great Sculptor, hew and polish us ; nor let,
    Hidden and lost, thy form within us lie.

Spare not the stroke; do with us as Thou wilt ;
    Let there be naught unfinish'd, broken, marr'd ;
Complete Thy purpose, that we may become
    Thy perfect image, O our God and Lord.
                HORATIUS BONAR

MY GOD, I LOVE THEE

MY God, I love Thee ! not because
 I hope for heaven thereby ;
Nor because those who love Thee not
 Must burn eternally.

Thou, O my Jesus, Thou didst me
 Upon the cross embrace !
For me didst bear the nails and spear,
 And manifold disgrace.

And griefs and torments numberless,
 And sweat of agony,
Yes, death itself—and all for one
 That was Thine enemy.

Then why, O blessed Jesus Christ,
 Should I not love Thee well ?
Not for the hope of winning heaven,
 Nor of escaping hell !

Not with the hope of gaining aught,
 Not seeking a reward ;
But as Thyself hath loved me,
 O ever-loving Lord !

E'en so I love Thee, and will love,
 And in Thy praise will sing—
Solely because Thou art my God,
 And my eternal King.

ST. FRANCIS XAVIER

Translated by Edward Caswall

"HE GIVETH HIS BELOVED SLEEP"

OF all the thoughts of God that are
    Borne inward unto souls afar,
  Along the Psalmist's music deep,
Now tell me if that any is
For gift or grace surpassing this—
  "He giveth his beloved sleep."

What would we give to our beloved?
The hero's heart, to be unmoved—
  The poet's star-tuned harp to sweep—
The senate's shout to patriot's vows—
The monarch's crown, to light the brows?
  "He giveth his beloved sleep."

O earth so full of dreary noises!
O men with wailing in your voices!
  O delved gold the wailers' heap!
O strife, O curse, that o'er it fall!
God makes a silence through you all,
  "And giveth his beloved sleep."

His dew drops mutely on the hill;
His cloud above it saileth still,
  Though on its slope men toil and reap.
More softly than the dew is shed,
Or cloud is floated overhead,
  "He giveth his beloved sleep."

ELIZABETH BARRETT BROWNING

THE INDWELLING SPIRIT

GOD is never so far off
 As even to be near.
He is within, our spirit is
 The home he holds most dear.

To think of him as by our side,
 Is almost as untrue
As to remove his throne beyond
 Those skies of starry blue.

So all the while I thought myself
 Homeless, forlorn and weary,
Missing my joy, I walked the earth
 Myself God's sanctuary.
FREDERICK WILLIAM FABER

PRAYER

PRAYER is the soul's sincere desire,
 Uttered or unexpressed—
The motion of a hidden fire
 That trembles in the breast.

Prayer is the burthen of a sigh,
 The falling of a tear—
The upward glancing of an eye,
 When none but God is near.
JAMES MONTGOMERY

NATURE

AS a fond mother, when the day is o'er,
    Leads by the hand her little child to bed,
Half-willing, half-reluctant to be led,
And leave his broken playthings on the floor,
Still gazing at them through the open door,
    Nor wholly reassured and comforted
    By promises of others in their stead,
Which though more splendid may not please him
        more ;
So Nature deals with us, and takes away
    Our playthings one by one, and by the hand
Leads us to rest so gently, that we go
Scarce knowing if we wish to go or stay,
    Being too full of sleep to understand
    How far the unknown transcends the what we know.

HENRY WADSWORTH LONGFELLOW

THE PROBLEM

NOT from a vain or shallow thought
    His awful Jove young Phidias brought ;
Never from lips of cunning fell
The thrilling Delphic oracle ;
Out from the heart of Nature rolled
The burdens of the Bible old ;
The litanies of nature came,

The Problem

Like the volcano's tongue of flame,
Up from the burning core below—
The canticles of love and woe :
The hand that rounded Peter's dome,
And groined the aisles of Christian Rome,
Wrought in a sad sincerity ;
Himself from God he could not free ;
He builded better than he knew ;—
The conscious stone to beauty grew.

Know'st thou what wove yon woodbird's nest
Of leaves, and feathers from her breast ?
Or how the fish outbuilt her shell,
Painting with morn each annual cell ?
Or how the sacred pine-tree adds
To her old leaves new myriads ?
Such and so grew these holy piles,
Whilst love and terror laid the tiles.
Earth proudly wears the Parthenon,
As the best gem upon her zone ;
And morning opes with haste her lids
To gaze upon the pyramids ;
O'er England's abbeys bends the sky,
As on its friends, with kindred eye ;
For out of thought's interior sphere
These wonders rose to upper air ;
And nature gladly gave them place,
Adopted them into her race,
And granted them an equal date
With Andes and with Ararat.

The Overflowing Cup

These temples grew as grows the grass—
Art might obey, but not surpass.
The passive Master lent his hand
To the vast soul that o'er him planned ;
And the same power that reared the shrine
Bestrode the tribes that knelt within.
Ever the fiery Pentecost
Girds with one flame the countless host,
Trances the heart through chanting choirs,
And through the priest the mind inspires.

RALPH WALDO EMERSON

THE OVERFLOWING CUP

INTO the crystal chalice of the soul
    Is falling, drop by drop, Life's blending mead.
The pleasant waters of our childhood speed
And enter first ; and Love pours in its whole
Deep flood of tenderness and gall.   There roll
    The drops of sweet and bitter that proceed
    From wedded trustfulness, and hearts that bleed
For children that outrun us to the goal.
And later come the calmer joys of age—
    The restful streams of quietude that flow
Around their fading lives, whose heritage
    Is whitened locks and voice serene and low.
These added blessings round the vessel up—
Death is the overflowing of the cup.

ANDREW RICE SAXTON

THE WAYSIDE CROSS

WAS it to my spirit's gain or loss,
　　One bright and balmy morning, as I went
From Liege's lovely environs to Ghent,
If hard by the wayside I found a cross,
That made me breathe a prayer upon the spot—
While Nature of herself, as if to trace
The emblem's use, had trailed around its base
The blue significant Forget-Me-Not?
Methought, the claims of charity to urge
More forcibly along with Faith and Hope,
The pious choice had pitch'd upon the verge
　　Of a delicious slope,
Giving the eye much variegated scope !—
" Look round," it whisper'd, " on that prospect rare,
Those vales so verdant and those hills so blue ;
Enjoy the sunny world, so fresh and fair,
But "—(how the simple legend pierc'd me thro' !)
　　" PRIEZ POUR LES MALHEUREUX."

.THOMAS HOOD
Ode to Rae Wilson, Esquire

THE ETERNAL GOODNESS

O FRIENDS ! with whom my feet have trod
    The quiet aisles of prayer,
Glad witness to your zeal for God
    And love of man I bear.

I trace your lines of argument ;
    Your logic linked and strong
I weigh as one who dreads dissent,
    And fears a doubt as wrong.

But still my human hands are weak
    To hold your iron creeds ;
Against the words ye bid me speak
    My heart within me pleads.

Who fathoms the Eternal Thought ?
    Who talks of scheme and plan ?
The Lord is God ! He needeth not
    The poor device of man.

I walk with bare, hushed feet the ground
    Ye tread with boldness shod ;
I dare not fix with mete and bound
    The love and power of God.

Ye praise His justice ; even such
    His pitying love I deem :
Ye seek a king ; I fain would touch
    The robe that hath no seam.

The Eternal Goodness

Ye see the curse that overbroods
   A world of pain and loss ;
I hear our Lord's beatitudes
   And prayer upon the cross.

   .   .   .   .

I see the wrong that round me lies,
   I feel the guilt within ;
I hear, with groan and travail-cries,
   The world confess its sin.

Yet, in the maddening maze of things,
   And tossed by storm and flood,
To one fixed trust my spirit clings ;
   I know that God is good !

   .   .   .   .

And so beside the Silent Sea
   I wait the muffled oar ;
No harm from Him can come to me
   On ocean or on shore.

I know not where His islands lift
   Their fronded palms in air ;
I only know I cannot drift
   Beyond His love and care.

O brothers ! if my faith is vain,
   If hopes like these betray,
Pray for me that my feet may gain
   The sure and safer way.

Crossing the Bar

And Thou, O Lord! by whom are seen
   Thy creatures as they be,
Forgive me if too close I lean
   My human heart on Thee!

JOHN GREENLEAF WHITTIER

CROSSING THE BAR

SUNSET and evening star,
   And one clear call for me!
And may there be no moaning of the bar,
   When I put out to sea,

But such a tide as moving seems asleep,
   Too full for sound and foam,
When that which drew from out the boundless deep
   Turns again home.

Twilight and evening bell,
   And after that the dark!
And may there be no sadness of farewell,
   When I embark;

For tho' from out our bourne of Time and Place
   The flood may bear me far,
I hope to see my Pilot face to face
   When I have cross'd the bar.

ALFRED, LORD TENNYSON

ALL'S WELL

PROPHETIC Hope, thy fine discourse
　　　Foretold not half life's good to me ;
Thy painter, Fancy, hath not force
　To show how sweet it is to be !
　　Thy witching dream
　　And pictured scheme
To match the fact still want the power ;
　　Thy promise brave
　　From birth to grave
Life's bloom may beggar in an hour.

Ask and receive,—'tis sweetly said ;
　Yet what to plead for I know not ;
For wish is worsted, Hope o'ersped,
　And aye to thanks returns my thought.
　　If I would pray,
　　I've nought to say
But this, that God may be God still,
　　For Him to live
　　Is still to give,
And sweeter than my wish his will.

O wealth of life beyond all bound !
　Eternity each moment given !

213

All's Well

What plummet may the Present sound ?
  Who promises a *future* heaven ?
    Or glad, or grieved,
    Oppressed, relieved,
In blackest night, or brightest day,
    Still pours the flood
    Of golden good,
And more than heartfull fills me aye.

My wealth is common ; I possess
  No petty province, but the whole ;
What's mine alone is mine far less
  Than treasure shared by every soul.
    Talk not of store,
    Millions or more—
Of values which the purse may hold,—
    But this divine !
    I own the mine
Whose grains outweigh a planet's gold.

I have a stake in every star,
  In every beam that fills the day ;
All hearts of men my coffers are,
  My ores arterial tides convey ;
    The fields, the skies,
    The sweet replies
Of thought to thought are my gold-dust,—
    The oaks, the brooks,
    And speaking looks
Of lovers' faith and friendship's trust.

All's Well

Life's youngest tides joy-brimming flow
  For him who lives above all years,
Who all-immortal makes the Now,
  And is not ta'en in Time's arrears,
    His life's a hymn
    The seraphim
Might hark to hear or help to sing,
    And to his soul
    The boundless whole
Its beauty all doth daily bring.

" All mine is thine," the sky-soul saith ;
  " The wealth I am must thou become ;
Richer and richer, breath by breath,—
  Immortal gain, immortal room ! "
    And since all His
    Mine also is,
Life's gift outruns my fancy far,
    And drowns the dream
    In larger stream,
As morning drinks the morning star.
                    DAVID ATWOOD WASSON

www.ingramcontent.com/pod-product-compliance
Lightning Source LLC
Chambersburg PA
CBHW030103030726
47498CB00007B/2237